PRAISE FOR
THE RHEA JENSEN SERIES:

5 OUT OF 5 STARS. AT THE TOP OF ITS GENRE ... PRATT'S WRITING STYLE IS MORE FUN THAN GRAFTON'S.

–JENNIE HANSEN, AUTHOR AND MERIDIAN REVIEWER
WWW.JENNIELHANSEN.COM

MYSTERY, ROMANCE, ACTION, MORMONS ... THIS BOOK HAS EVERYTHING!

–AMANDA DICKSON, KSL 102.7 AND AUTHOR OF CHANGE IT UP!
AMANDADICKSON.COM

33% MORE SASS ... SAME GREAT PRICE!

–REBECCA CRESSMAN, FM100

IF THE RHEA JENSEN SERIES BECOMES A MOVIE, I WANT TO WRITE THE THEME SONG!

–JON SCHMIDT, COMPOSER/PIANIST
WWW.JONSCHMIDT.COM

CLEVER, WITTY, SASSY ... THIS FAST-PACED BOOK WILL KEEP YOU READING INTO THE NIGHT AND LEAVING YOU CRAVING FOR MORE.

–RACHAEL RENEE ANDERSON, AUTHOR OF LUCK OF THE DRAW
RACHAELRENEEANDERSON.BLOGSPOT.COM

THE RHEA JENSEN SERIES

BOOK 4

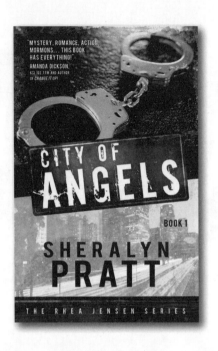

THE RHEA JENSEN SERIES

BOOK 4

SHERALYN
PRATT

BONNEVILLE BOOKS
SPRINGVILLE, UTAH

The views expressed within this work are the sole responsibility of the author and do not necessarily reflect the position of Cedar Fort, Inc., or any other entity.

This is a work of fiction. The characters, names, incidents, places, and dialogue are products of the author's imagination, and are not to be construed as real.

No part of this book may be reproduced in any form whatsoever, whether by graphic, visual, electronic, film, microfilm, tape recording, or any other means, without prior written permission of the publisher, except in the case of brief passages embodied in critical reviews and articles.

ISBN 13: 978-1-59955-425-9

Published by Bonneville Books, an imprint of Cedar Fort, Inc., 2373 W. 700 S., Springville, UT 84663
Distributed by Cedar Fort, Inc., www.cedarfort.com

LIBRARY OF CONGRESS CATALOGING-IN-PUBLICATION DATA

Pratt, Sheralyn.
kaysville / Sheralyn Pratt.
  p. cm.
 Originally published: Salt Lake City, Utah : Spectrum Books, c2003.
 ISBN 978-1-59955-425-9 (alk. paper)
 1. Women private investigators—Fiction. 2. Embezzlement—Fiction. 3. Mormon missionaries—Fiction. I. Title.

PS3616.R3846S67 2010
813'.6—dc22   b095 8518 7/16

2010005457

Cover design by Angela D. Olsen
Cover design © 2010 by Lyle Mortimer
Edited and typeset by Megan E. Welton

Printed in the United States of America

10 9 8 7 6 5 4 3 2 1

To my muse . . . I hope I got it right.

ACKNOWLEDGMENTS

There are three people who need huge shout-outs for this book being half as good as it is. Jessica, thanks for being the first on board in loving Kay as much as I do, and always being willing to talk fashion and snobbery with me. Elizabeth, thank you for being the Southern soul you are and schooling me on the South. And Viola . . . yes, you, Viola, for always giving me the straight talk when it comes to fashion dos and taboos. Without you I would have ugly hair and a single digit fashion IQ, instead of merely a double digit one. Love you more than you know!

ONE

T-MINUS TWENTY HOURS till my parents disowned me. In the meantime, there was a wedding to throw and a coyote to kill. I might be disinherited as soon as the last guest left my brother's reception that night, but I still needed to pull my weight.

And this coyote needed to show up.

So far he'd poached a baker's dozen of my Mama's Grand Champion hens without so much as us spying him once. He had a knack for knowing when he was being watched, it seemed. And by his tracks, it was clear he made his move an hour or so before the sun came up—before anything was up, really.

Because of him, I'd slept in grubby camo, propped against the trunk of a poplar tree on a rise above the coop. Mama might sob to the congregation that I'd forsaken Jesus and sold my soul to embrace the sins of the world, but she'd never be able to say that I didn't save her precious hens from the most cunning coyote Monroe County had ever seen.

This was my last shot at the little devil, and I had my .30-30 Winchester to make sure I did the job right. My brothers had proven that he didn't fall for bait. Every time they sweetened the coop, he wouldn't show. So we'd gotten up early a few mornings and waited for him, but he didn't show then either.

In my last-ditch effort, I'd set up shop about midnight and set my phone on silent, and I'd been staring at a whole lot of nothing ever since.

My stomach sank when a glow appeared on the eastern horizon. He should have showed by now. In my pocket, my phone glowed with a text from Jake.

The dang thing show yet? *it read.*

Not yet, *I typed back, trying not to feel completely bummed. I'd wanted to do this one thing for Mama before leaving for UCLA tomorrow morning.*

My phone lit up with another text. It's chilly out. You want me to come keep you warm? We could make out. =)

If Mama had her way, I'd do more than make out with the boy. I'd marry him and join together two of the richest families within a hundred miles. A Griswold-Eatonton wedding? Mama would surely fall out the moment the wedding march started.

Sorry. *I typed back.* I already have a date this morning, even if he does stand me up.

I'd known Jake all my life. Sure, in the last year he'd stopped treating me like a little sister and started looking at me with a glint in his eye that made me fidget, but kissing him was like locking lips with my own brother. I knew because I'd tried kissing Jake once. It'd been okay at first, but I'd lost it when Jake let out a weird little groan as he pulled me tight against him. As soon as that happened, I'd caught a case of the giggles and never quite recovered. Even as I lay in bed that night hours later, the memory had me shaking with laughter.

My phone glowed with yet another text. Aw, baby, why you huntin' coyotes when you could bag a fox?

Well wasn't he flirty before sunrise. There's no thrill to the hunt when the prey is willing, *I wrote back.*

As I pressed send, a motion caught my attention below, and then disappeared without a whisper of a sound. In one silent motion, I stashed my phone in a pocket and gripped my Winchester. My mind told me that seeing the movement was just wishful thinking, but the hammering of my heart told a different story. It was saying that my date had arrived, so I extended the rifle and used my non-shooting hand to stabilize it.

Several seconds passed before I caught action at my one o'clock about a hundred yards out, trotting through the shadows as arrogant as could be even as I tracked him with my scope. As if sensing the attention, he paused behind a line of brush. In the dim light I couldn't make out his outline, so I held position, waiting for him to cut over toward the chicken coop.

He took so long to move again that I wondered if I was waiting out a ghost, but then he made his move. He was faster than I thought, as if he knew he was taking a risk but couldn't pass up chicken dumplings. Leading the target's heart, I took a quick inhale. When I was sure I had his pace down, I let out a small exhale, found my moment of stillness, and squeezed the trigger.

All of nature jerked awake as my shot rang out, followed by a yelp. After a quick recoil, I watched in my scope as the coyote missed its next steps, hit the dirt, and grew still. One moment the beast was a cocky hunter, and the next he was laid out like a rug in my daddy's den.

Life. It freaked me out how fragile it was sometimes. If someone put me in his sites, I could be gone just as fast as that coyote. And then what? Mama always said that's when we'd meet Jesus, join the heavenly choirs, and praise God's name forever. If we were good. But if that was heaven, I might just be up for checking out hell. Anything had to be more interesting than an eternity of singing.

My phone started glowing again with a new text from Jake: I heard that.

I smiled, happy to have someone to share my victory with. Mama was a hard woman to please, but I knew she'd love this parting gift—even if she did damn me to hell for wanting something no refined woman should: a career. An education. Fame. Sinful things like that.

A preacher's daughter through and through, Mama raised me

on the strait and narrow, teaching me from day one exactly how tight of a rope Jesus wanted me to walk. Problem was, if I had to spend one more day being perfect, I might just scream out every profanity I'd never said in my life. Perfection wasn't an option for me anymore. I couldn't walk around seeing the world through a peephole. I wanted to see it all. The good, the bad, the ugly . . . everything!

And that meant leaving home.

It also unfortunately meant that Mama had sworn that she would not support a daughter in sin, and nor would her family. And when a Southern mama declares something, it's law. If I got on my flight tomorrow morning, I would lose everything I knew to go to a unfamiliar place where I wouldn't know a soul.

Mission accomplished, I typed to Jake even as my stomach twisted at the thought of leaving. *I'd miss him. A lot. In truth, Jake wouldn't make a bad husband once I got past the weirdness of having his hands and mouth on me. He was Mama's plan for me and the only way back into her good graces. If UCLA didn't work out, I could always fall back on marrying him and making my parents happy.*

But in the meantime, all I had to offer them was a new rug.

* * *

OCTOBER 2010

Law enforcement made quick work with the crime scene tape as I moved to my mark. Nick gave the camera one last adjustment before nodding that he was ready.

"Are we doing the teaser promo first?" he asked.

I nodded. "Ready."

The instructions of my image consultant, George, drummed through my head as I positioned myself for the shot. Posture slightly relaxed, weight forward, and the tripod raised four inches to make me look shorter.

Market research showed that I came across as arrogant to Utah viewers. My eyes, expressions, make-up, wardrobe, and posture had garnered some negative feedback, and George was my partner in getting Utah to like me.

Never in my life would I have ever thought winning the approval of Utahns would be a goal on my to-do list. If I thought about it too long I'd get a headache, so I just approached it in terms of pay scale. If my viewership liked me, I got a raise. Thinking about it that way made the situation less painful.

Power colors—including red, white, and black—had been banned from my broadcast wardrobe, which was why I'd purchased my Elie Tahari pant suit in deep merlot. That would probably be banned—along with my Louboutin platforms—but management would have to look me in the eye when they told me I looked too good to be an afternoon reporter.

Then I'd make them explain why they didn't stick me in prime time where I belonged.

Nick counted down, showing me the last two beats with only his fingers before the camera light came on.

"This is Kathryn McCoy, reporting to you live from Rose Park, where a woman was found shot to death this morning in her home. Tune in live at noon for this developing story." I held for two beats until the red light went dark.

"That's a cut," Nick said.

I repositioned a stray hair tickling against my neck. "Did I look appropriately humble?"

He nodded, pointing to my mouth. "The nude lipstick helps, and I think George is going to want to make you stay with the straight hair. It's less . . ." He paused, searching for the right word. ". . . Provocative."

That would be a pain, if true. Yes, my hair looked fantastic straight, but every day? "You're probably right. Grab more B-roll of them taping off the area and whatever else you can grab for voice over. I'm going to find out who our PIO is."

"Call me when you need me," Nick said, removing the large camera from its tripod.

"Of course." Moving to the broadcast van, I traded out my mic for a notebook and put on some contraband lip gloss. I'd remove it before the next broadcast, but for the moment I needed a man in uniform to stop what he was doing and talk to me. Shimmering lips helped.

Turning back to the crime scene, I scanned the crowd for familiar faces. I'd seen Detective Richards when we arrived, but he'd gone inside. The only uniforms still outside were the beat cops roping off the scene. I approached the one closest to me, and dispensed with the niceties, since I might only get one question out before he bolted.

"Who's talking to the media today?"

He wrapped the yellow tape once around the tree and started off. "Officer Dahl."

For a moment I thought he was kidding. Dahl was a trained Public Information Officer? If anyone hated a camera, it was Dahl. Plus, he had no particular rank to speak of. Had he been promoted? I hadn't seen him for about four weeks, not since the day I'd essentially made out with him under a giant arch of antlers in Jackson Hole. He'd proven talented at avoiding me ever since.

Yeah, interviewing him wouldn't be awkward at all.

I sighed, looking over the scene again. At least I knew who I was looking for. Six-foot-three, dark hair, chocolate eyes, broad chest, and biceps as big around as my thighs. Even with the five extra inches my Louboutins gave me, the man would still be an inch taller than me, which kind of defeated the purpose of wearing platforms at all.

Ken Dahl. As ridiculous as it was that his parents had named him that, he lived up to the name. So. Hot. If the guy were a little less tightly wound, he could be a model instead of a cop—or just play a cop on TV. But no, the guy was a Boy

Scout and straight shooter. Unfortunately.

It took me a second to find him because he wasn't actually on the scene but across the street looking up something on his cruiser's computer. I chose to ignore the catch in my breath as I spotted him as well as the fact that I pressed my lips together to make sure they were damp. Just because I'd kissed him the last time I saw him didn't mean I was going to kiss him this time. In fact, I definitely wasn't going to kiss him again, so I might as well get down to business.

Crossing the street, I made it half way to Dahl's cruiser before he spotted me. I saw him groan even though I couldn't hear it and got to his car by the time he stepped out of it.

"So, look who was secretly a PIO all this time," I teased, noting his suit and tie. As much as I didn't want to look, the man stretched Circle S slacks in all the right places. And while I wasn't the biggest fan of economy brands, his suit was a step up from the thousands of Mr. Mac suits I saw everywhere. "Lose a bet or something?"

He faltered, as if he'd been expecting me to say something else before he answered. "It's payback, I guess."

"For?" I prompted.

"Putting in my two-week notice. I have media duty until my last day."

Dahl? Leaving the police force? There was no reason for me to feel a moment of panic at the news, and yet I did. "Where are you going?"

"Church security," he said, trying to keep his tone casual even though the look in his eyes said there was nothing casual about this job. It was a happy change for him. "They finally let me in."

"Congratulations." What else could I say? "So will I see you around Temple Square then?"

"Not likely," he laughed, before corralling us back on track. "But you didn't come over to talk about this."

"No." I glanced over to the house. "Have you been inside?"

"Yeah." No elaboration, though I hadn't expected much from him.

"How many shots were fired?"

"Just one to the head," he confirmed. "They're thinking it might be a suicide."

My face scrunched in disbelief before I could stop it. Dahl caught the look, so I decided to just say what I was thinking. "The woman was a wife and mother. A mom wouldn't shoot herself. She'd take pills and go to sleep or something a little more considerate for the kids. Men blow their heads off without caring who does the clean up. Mothers don't."

"If you say so. I'm just telling you how things are right now."

Fair enough. "Has the family been notified?"

Dahl nodded, flipping open his cell phone to check something I couldn't see. "The husband and sister have been notified. Neither is on scene yet. ETA for the husband is twenty minutes."

Good to know. "Does he want to talk to the media?"

Dahl shut his cruiser's door and started to walk away. "I can't imagine he does, but I'm sure you'll bat your eyelashes and get an interview anyway."

I trailed after him, not letting his intended insult sink in. "It's called doing my job."

He picked up his pace. "Yeah? Well, I'm going to do mine. Nice seeing you again."

I ignored the blatant blow off. "Great. I'll get my cameraman over here and we'll set up the shot."

Dahl turned and poised himself for another dismissal before realizing I was right. He was the media liaison and, as such, was required to give me an interview so I didn't bother anyone else. And I could be a pain when I chose to be.

"Like it or not, you owe me a few sound bytes, Dahl."

Nick saved me a phone call by showing up with both his camera and the tripod. The crafty guy had even stashed my mic in his back pocket. I'd been training him well. Behind Nick, the reporter from Channel 13 came to snag Dahl, and I sent her a territorial look. The great and marvelous Mindy Gibbons, dressed in Ross's finest—no-name shoes, a Willi Smith top, and a random skirt with an awful gold rope necklace that belonged on a woman twice her age.

She looked exactly like what she was: an underpaid professional who doubled as a thrifty shopper in her downtime. Her ensemble actually hurt to look at.

"He's mine first," I warned her, and she came to a halt. Not because of me but because of Dahl. The fact that he sent her a smile did not escape me. He'd given me nothing but stony looks, and now Mindy was getting flashes of his perfect teeth, amazing bone structure, and flirty eyes?

"Hey, Mindy," he called to her. "I'll be right over."

He was volunteering to interview with Mindy and calling her by name? Proving he was capable of being nice to other women while dismissing me totally rubbed wrong. If this was how he treated all the women he kissed, then it was no wonder he was divorced . . . and single.

"You two share a pew or something?" I muttered, leading him to where Nick was setting up.

"What was that?" he asked, moving even with me.

"Nothing."

"Didn't sound like nothing," he countered.

"And since when do you care?" I shot back just as we reached Nick, and I decided it was better to talk to him. "Officer Dahl is tall and wide, so let's find a mark where he doesn't block the background."

Nick looked back and forth between the tops of our heads.

"Sure. Anyone got a step ladder?" he quipped. Without my heels, Nick was still an inch shorter than me—the exact height of my friend's fiancé, Ty. At the moment, he came up to my and Dahl's chins.

"What if we stand in the gutter and you take high ground?" I offered, touching Dahl's arm to indicate he should step down.

"I got it," Dahl said, moving his arm out of reach while stepping down. Nick saw the move and sent me a veiled look. The boy was going to have some questions for me after all this.

"Let's start with you right here," I said, motioning Dahl in closer. He hesitated as if looking for an option in which he could stand six feet away from me for an interview, so I dropped my notebook on the ground. "There. Use that as your mark and stand right behind it."

I knew why he was hesitating. I felt it too—that strange hum of tension. But were we still in high school? No. We were grown adults on the clock, and a woman had been killed a hundred feet from where we stood. The world could really care less about mine and Dahl's chemistry.

He stepped behind the notebook, leaving a solid two feet between us, and I made a point of reaching over to angle his body slightly. "You need to stand here so the background is right. These are for promos, so I won't be in the frame." I moved to my approximate mark. "I'll be here holding the mic out to you."

"Holy crap," Nick said, backing away. "I can't see past him at all. He's like a human wall."

"We'll hold still while you adjust." I said that more for Dahl than Nick, since the guy looked ready to bolt now that I was closer than arm's length. Such conspicuous discomfort would be amusing if it weren't completely counterproductive. "Do you have a prepared statement, or do you want me to ask questions?"

"Statement."

Oh, we were down to one-word responses already? Nice. "Are you releasing her name?"

"Yes. Julia Hernandez." He was avoiding eye contact, which was fine on personal time, but he'd look like a pouty child if he did this on camera. I needed to fix it and quick.

"Have you sent a picture to media?" I asked.

He indicated his car. "Just did. Scanned and sent."

I brought my phone up to see if it had appeared in my inbox yet. Nothing so far. The news release desk probably just hadn't forwarded it yet.

"What are you doing?" Dahl asked.

"Texting your boss to tell him you suck at being a media liaison."

He let out a little huff. "He already knows that."

"Yeah, but I don't think he knows exactly how bad you are." I put the phone back in my pocket and glanced back at Nick who was adjusting the focus. We were almost done with this nightmare. None of us spoke while Dahl stood like a man facing a firing squad. He looked horrible.

"Seriously, Dahl, are you going to be this stiff when the camera turns on?" I sent a pointed look to Mindy who was hovering about twenty feet away so she could listen in when we recorded. "Here's a PR pointer for you: you can't be closed-mouthed and dismissive to one station and all but give air kisses to the competition."

"That's not what I'm doing," he snapped.

"No offense, officer," Nick cut in. "But you totally are."

I could have kissed Nick but turned back to Dahl. "And unless you swallow that chip on your shoulder in the next few seconds, I'm going to have recorded proof to show your boss. You may only have two weeks left on the force, but how about we make them good weeks?"

His eyes narrowed. "Maybe I'm nicer to Mindy because she's not such a pain."

Wow. The only way he could sound more petty would be if he stomped his feet while he said that. I raised an eyebrow at him, letting him know that he was officially crossing to my bad side. "This is business, not *The Bachelor*. Ask her out on your own time, but don't be confused as to why we're all here. I'm talking to you because you represent the police department right now, and I have a job to do." I turned back to Nick. "We got the shot?"

"Yes, but is that lip gloss I see?"

I'd forgotten about that. "We'll do my part after the officer here has moved on to greener pastures. This will just be Dahl's prepared statement about the murder."

"It hasn't been ruled a murder," Dahl corrected.

"Not yet. But it will be," I said with confidence.

Dahl wasn't going to let me have the last word. "The shot was point blank."

Good to know. I squared off with him. "You really think it was a suicide?"

He nodded. "Evidence supports it."

"Willing to bet on it?"

I might as well have slapped him. "That's immoral!"

I could have gagged on his self-righteousness. "Uh-huh. As immoral as kissing?"

Dahl actually flinched at my reference to what we were both tiptoeing around, and I saw bells go off in Nick's head. I'd have told him in the van anyway.

"Twenty bucks says it's murder," I said before Dahl could respond to my kissing reference.

"I'm not betting on something like that."

"Fine." I turned back to the camera. "Let's do this."

Nick nodded, fighting a smile. "Ready when you are."

"Oh, I'm definitely ready." I turned my body to face Dahl's again and snagged his arm before he could step back. "Stay right where you are," I cooed. "One sound byte and you're free, so let's try to get it on take one."

Dahl said nothing. I flipped the mic on and did a sound

check—hating the sick feeling in the pit of my stomach like I'd done something wrong. But hadn't I started off nice? Playful, even? Why should I feel guilty when he was the one making this obligatory interaction unpleasant?

"Levels are good," Nick said, holding up his hand with all five fingers extended. "Recording in five, four, three—" He ticked off two and one with his hands before the light blinked on.

"We are on scene with Officer Dahl of the Salt Lake Police Department. Officer, can you walk us through what happened this morning?"

I held out the mic to him and gave him a nod. To my utter joy, he did not clam up.

"At 10:17 this morning, officers responded to a reports of shots fired at the home of Julia and Abel Hernandez. Upon arrival, the officers discovered the body of Julia Hernandez, who had been shot once in the head. We know that her husband was at work during the time of the shooting and can say that he is not a person of interest at this time. The two Hernandez children were removed from school and informed about the tragic loss of their mother. They are currently in their father's custody as we investigate this case further."

Not bad. "Do you have any suspects?"

"Currently no eyewitnesses have stepped forward claiming to see anyone fleeing the scene, but we are actively investigating all possibilities and encourage anyone with information regarding the tragic events of this morning to call in tips to the number on your screen."

I brought the mic back to me. "Was the murder weapon found at the scene?"

He didn't even blink. "Due to the nature of the case, I cannot release that information at this time."

And he wasn't going to release any other information, either. If he were anyone else, I would have pushed for more.

But this was Dahl, and I knew this was all he had to say. I'd get others to fill in Dahl's tight-lipped gap. I turned to Nick and waved my finger in a circle to let him know I was done. He gave me a confused look, but the camera light went dark.

"There," I said to Dahl. "Wasn't that painless?"

He stepped away. "If you say so."

I flashed him my usual smile. "Thank you for your time, officer. We really appreciate it. Don't let us hold you up any more."

He nodded, stepping away and over to Mindy. I watched him go while Nick joined me.

"That was . . . um . . . interesting."

"Yeah," I agreed, noting that Dahl reached out to shake Mindy's hand. Such a simple gesture shouldn't have me seeing red, but it did. The guy all but cried bloody murder if I brushed up again him. "Twenty bucks says she's Mormon."

"Mindy? Oh, she totally is," Nick said. "That's no secret. Why do you care?"

My mouth literally tasted of acid. "It's like a little club. If you're not in, then you're out."

"Sure," Nick teased. "Or maybe his behavior has more to do with the fact that you two have a history."

"Once," I clarified, holding up a finger. "We kissed once, and it wasn't a romantic thing. It was like . . . kissing someone at New Year's. Not personal."

His lips pursed as he failed to hide his smile. "Oh, it looks personal to me."

"Whatever," I grumbled and walked back to the van so I wouldn't have to watch Mindy adjust Dahl's necktie before her interview.

THE LAST WEDDING guest had left about two hours ago, and the house was still. It'd been nice to see everyone and say good-bye without really saying good-bye. It was my brother's day, after all, not mine.

Looking around at everything that wouldn't fit in my suitcase, the pangs of homesickness set in before I'd even taken a step out the door. I'd known straight off that I'd miss things like my horse, Lady, but would my parents keep my barrel racing and vaulting trophies? My saddle and guns? My poster signed by Faith Hill and the quilt Nana made? What would happen to them?

The collage of news stories on the wall over my bed would certainly be stripped down and burned, but that didn't worry me. They'd served their purpose. What I'd really miss were the small things, like the view of my family's orchard from my bedroom window.

I walked to the windowpane one last time, seeing only vague silhouettes in the dim lighting of a new moon. The view looked more like a picture—not even a puff of wind moved in the night. It was as if the air slept along with everyone else in the house I might never see again.

My heart clutched and my courage failed momentarily just as a light knock came on my door.

"It's three," Jake whispered. "Time to get going if you don't want to miss your flight."

Stepping away from the window, I moved to get my bag only to have Jake grab it a second before me.

"You're not in Los Angeles yet," he teased. "I hear men make women carry their own luggage there, but I was raised better."

Despite his lanky build, he picked up the bag as if it were a folding chair rather than fifty pounds of personal items. Our eyes caught in the dim light.

"I'll miss you," I blurted before I could think better of it.

He didn't smile. "And I'll confess that when I offered to take you to the airport, there's no way I thought you'd actually be going." He put my bag down and stepped in. Close. "Stay, Katie. Los Angeles doesn't have anything for you. Let me take care of you. What do you want that I can't give?"

Did he want a list? Because it was a long one, but before I could say a word back his lips were on mine. And this time it was different from the last. I didn't laugh. I didn't even want to. Maybe it was how he was holding me this time that made the difference. I didn't even notice what our lips were doing because I was shocked at how his arms locked me into his body as if he never wanted to let go. It was like he needed me or something.

When he pulled away, Jake's grip stayed strong even though his eyes didn't seem to focus right. "I mean it, Katie. Say the word, and we'll set the date for your granddad to marry us."

I couldn't think of a girl I knew who wouldn't swoon if Jake Eatonton spoke those words to her. Yet somehow he'd uttered them to the one girl who wasn't in love with him. I knew I had to say no, but there was no need to be harsh about it.

"Jake, you know I've got to try this. When I think of the future, I just don't see myself here."

Jake stepped away. "That's just silliness. Why would you want to go to a jammed-up city where no one knows anyone and acid falls from the sky? Might as well move into an armpit."

"I might come back," I said without knowing why. Reaching between us, I gripped his hand. "If I do, you'll be the first to know. I swear."

I watched his jaw flex and knew he was fighting back something else he wanted to say. Instead he simply dropped my hand and grabbed the suitcase again.

"We're losing time," he said and turned for the door.

* * *

Julia Hernandez's husband, Abel, provided a much more compelling interview. He spoke on and on about what a beautiful, giving person his wife was and how he had no idea how something like this would happen. She'd been happy and normal when he left that morning.

Nick got it all on tape with his consent. Abel was devastated and shell shocked. More than that, he wanted to let the whole world know that his wife had been a wonderful, selfless woman and a fantastic mother. Then, when the police let him see her body, he fell apart.

"I'd guess it's a safe bet that he's innocent," Nick said quietly so only I could hear after the man vomited on his front lawn.

"Definitely," I agreed, just as a curvy Latino woman sprinted down the sidewalk toward us. I gave Nick's arm a little tap and motioned toward her. "I think someone just got the news."

"Neighbor?"

From the woman's tear-stained face and panicked expression, it was clear she was more. "Friend, I think. Get ready."

The woman didn't even hesitate when she reached the yellow tape. She broke through it like a first place finisher and made it about five steps before two officers intercepted her.

"This is a crime scene, ma'am. We need you to step back behind the tape."

Stout as the woman may have been, she fought like a frenzied tank with claws. "I need to see Julia. She's my best friend! I won't believe she's dead until I see her."

"I'm sorry, but we cannot let you inside, ma'am."

Lunging toward the house as if her life depended on it, the woman actually succeeded in taking one of the officers down and probably would have gotten past the other one if three new officers hadn't joined in the mix. Wailing, she pushed her body to the house even as officers dragged her away.

I could relate. I had a best friend too. And if I ever got news that Rhea had died, I'd shoot my way through a crowd of officers to get to her.

Forget the husband or the cops. I was looking at the only person worth interviewing when it came to finding out what really happened at 10:17 that morning, and I needed to calm her down before she got herself put into police custody.

Moving in, I approached the friend through her line of sight and focused on her eyes. In the brief moment where a flash of confusion overcame her panic, I spoke.

"What's your name?" I asked, my voice calm and the words overly enunciated in case she couldn't hear over the officers.

She blinked, her struggles stopping for a brief moment, and I held my hand up to encourage that she not start up again. "Maria," she said, even though I only saw the word over the officers yelling for her to calm down. I looked over the officers, recognized one, and moved in.

"Officer Rhodes," I called into the chaos and he actually looked at me. "If you can get her across the street, I promise I'll calm her down."

He turned his attention back to Maria as if I hadn't spoken at all.

"Maria," I said over all of them, and she stopped struggling. She stood where she was, breathing like a perplexed, rabid animal. "If the officers let you come with me, will you promise to stay outside the yellow tape?"

After a few awkward beats, she nodded.

"If you try to get to the house again, they're going to have to arrest you. And that means you won't see Julia until tomorrow at the soonest."

A quiet sob escaped her, but she nodded. I looked at the officers and motioned for them to let her go. No one wanted an arrest here. There wasn't a single thing to be gained by it, and these officers knew it.

"We'll head across the street and stay where you can see us," I said to them.

The officers shared a look, released her, and stepped away. I held out my hand. "Maria, do you want to come with me?"

For a scary moment it looked like she might run for the house again, but then she took a step toward me. "Let's go."

Turning to the street, we walked side by side toward Dahl's cruiser. I glanced over at Nick and motioned for him not to join us yet. Maria and I had some chatting to do before we introduced a camera.

"Why'd you do that?" she said, casting me a suspicious look. "What do you want from me?"

The woman would sense a lie a mile away, so I just came out with the truth. "I want to know who killed your best friend and why."

"You don't care," she snapped, looking over my blonde hair, blue eyes, and fair skin. "Not really."

In a bold move, I grabbed her by the shoulder and whipped her around to face me while she was mid-step. "Seriously? Look me in the eye and explain to me how I don't care when I just saved you from getting hauled to jail. Do you seriously believe it doesn't affect me when a woman gets shot in her own home because I'm white?"

Oh yeah, I went there. But in her own subtle way, Maria had gone there first and needed to be called out on it.

"I've seen you on TV," she sneered, getting up in my face as best she could considering our height difference. "You only cover the bad stuff. The Latino community does a lot of good too, and all you talk about is when one of us shoots someone."

"Or gets shot," I said, gesturing to Julia's house and not denying her accusation. "I care about your friend losing her life, Maria. And I'm going to do everything I can to find out what happened here this morning. And to do that, I need you."

"I don't even know if my friend is dead. They won't let me see her!"

"No, they won't," I confirmed. "Probably not until after the autopsy."

"But I need to see!"

"Why?" I asked softly, sensing the answer was important, and suddenly Maria had nothing to say. Odd. "Why do you need to see her body, Maria?"

"Because I don't believe it!" She yelled the words, which only made it all the more obvious that she did believe her friend was dead.

"I'm sorry, Maria, but she is. Julia is gone."

Suddenly, her arms were around me in a hug of vice-like strength. She buried her face into my breast with an intimacy I wasn't quite sure what to do with and sobbed into my outfit. I could only hope she wasn't wearing mascara.

"It's not possible. It can't be," she chanted repeatedly, holding on to me as though I was Julia. I saw a few people eyeing us, including Mindy, but they all kept their distance.

"Do you know who killed her, Maria?"

And just like that, the crying stopped. I'd hit on something. I knew it just as surely as I knew she wouldn't tell me a thing. I needed to backpedal and win a little trust.

"Maria, would you like to be interviewed for the news and tell everyone the good things about Julia? The more people care, the more likely we are to catch her killer."

Pulling away to look her in the eye, I saw something unexpected. Fear. Something I had just said had scared the attitude right out of her. And whatever it was, she wasn't going to share it with a blonde-haired, blue-eyed white woman wearing an ensemble that would cost her several paychecks. I needed to get her on TV so she would know I was for real.

"My cameraman, Nick, is right over there. Do you see him?" Nick gave a little wave as I pointed him out. "All I want is for you to tell the world what a great friend Julia is." Present tense, not past tense. I didn't want her freaking out again. "Tell the community all the good things she's done for Salt Lake. Can you do that?"

She looked over Nick's curly dark hair and tanned skin. I didn't know if had any Latino in him, but in that moment I was just glad he didn't look like the Aryan ideal.

"I can do that," she said at last. "Yeah, I have plenty to say about that."

I didn't doubt that for one second. I just hoped that ten seconds of her speech would be good enough for a thumbs-up from my producer.

THREE

I OFFICIALLY LIVED IN *a place where no one would look twice at me if I walked down the street half naked. Double-takes were reserved for worn-in jeans and boots that had actually set foot in a pasture. As it turned out, by Hollywood standards, every article of clothing I'd brought along didn't do me any favors in the first impression department.*

Slouching in the back row of my investigative journalism class, I watched as other students filtered into the auditorium for the first day of class. The girls looked like magazine ads. What threw me off was that the guys were beautiful too. Soft, but hard at the same time, their sculpted bodies contrasted with soft hands as if to say that their muscles were for decoration only. In fact, everything seemed to be about decoration in L.A. Cars, clothes, hairdos, houses, jewelry—everything that normal people have, only much, much more.

A girl in a tight yellow shirt that said "Tune in Tokyo" headed for the center rows of seats. "Covering" the lower half of her body was a pair of shorts so short that her pockets hung out from underneath. Two girls entered behind her, side-by-side, both texting into their phones. Neither carried books, but one of them did have a Chihuahua in her purse. Behind them were models for hippy chic in their pristine tie-dye and styled grunge hair.

Did everyone just wake up with a sheen of gloss on them in California? Was it something in the water? If so, I needed to drink up.

While watching one of the hippy girls and wondering how she got her curls so static free, another student walked in. I felt him before I saw him, and when I looked up, my jaw literally dropped. He was tall—really tall. Probably four inches taller than me in my boots. And while he had the whole Hollywood sheen going on just like everyone else, it didn't make him any less of a bad boy. I'd met my fair share of bad boys, but they'd all been cut from the same cloth—rodeo cloth.

This boy represented a whole new cloth.

My mind blanked as I realized that I could actually feel my pulse pounding in my throat. That was a first. So were the sweaty hands that I usually only got before a competition. No boy had ever had me drying my hands on my pants before, and we'd only been in the same room for a matter of seconds. The human body truly was a marvel.

I cleared my throat and kept my eyes glued on him until he turned back to the entrance and said something to the person entering behind him.

She looked like . . . well, I wasn't sure what she looked like, but she was gorgeous. In a tank and jeans, there was no denying the girl was an athlete. Her dark hair contrasted with ice-blue eyes so vivid it seemed they belonged to a creature from the animal kingdom, not a human. Her skin glowed a deep bronze that looked like it might be naturally dark beneath her tan. Her eyes fascinated me the most. I wanted those eyes. Not the color per se—I would look like a freak with them—but the look behind them. This girl looked like she had seen everything there was to see and had grown rather bored with it all.

Within two seconds of entering the room, those iceberg eyes had sized everyone up, including me. When she caught me looking at her, the frost in her gaze had me looking down at my notebook before I realized I wasn't the type of person who shied away from eye contact. But by the time I looked back, she had moved on, and I'd missed the moment.

Watching her move to the front of the room, I wasn't savvy enough to discern the style of her clothes, but they looked tailored and sophisticatedly casual. I swallowed and slumped down a little in my chair, feeling more out of place than ever.

Three more normal-looking guys came in a few moments later and joined the hot couple in the third row. When the girl sat, each of the guys took a seat around her—all clearly not interested in talking to anyone but one another. I paid attention when the teacher called role. The hot guy was named Ben Stone and his girl-friend was Rhea Jensen. The other three guys were Isaac, Aaron, and Danny.

Five names I knew I would never forget.

* * *

At 3:01 p.m., I exited the front entrance of my condo and spotted Rhea's Audi. The girl was obscenely punctual, even if it was only to pick me up for a Tuesday evening of horseback riding. Leaving at three put us ahead of rush hour and gave me and Rhea plenty of daylight to work with.

Gone were my work clothes, and in their place were original-cut Wranglers, an olive tank, and some Lucchese cowboy boots. No designer could lay claim to my belt and buckle, though. Those had both been handmade by my dad and were timeless. I'd swept my sleek news 'do into a simple ponytail and applied a soft pink on my lips to complete the look.

Firing up her engine the moment she saw me, Rhea's Audi R8 had the instant attention of every male on the block. True, neither my bank account or my environmental sensibilities would allow me to buy a sports car, but that didn't mean I didn't like the rush of driving shotgun and watching men crane their necks for a better look. Too bad for them that the woman behind the wheel was just as far out of their league as the actual car was.

"That just doesn't get old, does it?" I asked, opening the door.

"Never will," she agreed. As little as Rhea Jensen tried to look good these days, I still found myself taking fashion cues from her. I, for example, would never even think to try on sunglasses designed by J Lo, but they looked flawless on Rhea, as did her boot-cut jeans and Fruit of the Loom tank. Her statement piece was her turquoise inlay western boots, meant more for Carrie Underwood to wear on stage at a concert than for riding in an actual pasture. And, of course, the turquoise on her boots matched the shade on her belt and accents on her sunglasses exactly.

The girl could turn white trash into red carpet as easy as breathing.

"Nice glasses," I said, taking my seat and reaching for the seat belt.

"They work," was all she had to say while checking her mirrors. "Looks like you had a busy day today."

"Insane," I agreed as she pulled into traffic. "Guess who's quitting the police force?"

She raised an eyebrow. "Dahl got the Church security job?"

How did she know that? "Yep. He's got two more weeks and then he's off to do whatever those guys do."

Her lips pursed as she pointed us to the freeway. "It'll be good for him. He's the type."

"Got that right," I snorted, hoping she wouldn't ask how things went with him.

Rhea checked her rearview mirror, just like she did every ten seconds. "Interesting interview you got today."

My heart skipped a beat in joy. "Did you see it?"

"The friend?" she clarified, waiting for my nod. "What do you think she knows?"

"I think she knows who did it."

"If anyone does, it'd be her," Rhea agreed.

"The weird thing was, she was in complete denial when she heard Julia was dead. She said she wouldn't believe it was true until she physically saw the body."

Rhea had no quick response to that, and her face stayed placid as she thought through options. That was the best thing about her. I didn't have to explain anything to Rhea, although she'd listen if I felt like doing so anyway. Her inductive and deductive reasoning skills were off the charts, her instincts nearly always on the mark. And best of all, she didn't mind talking shop.

She counted her thoughts off with the fingers of one hand, while steering with the other. "Denial. Loyalty. Guilt. Devotion. Those are reasons to want to see a body, but I would guess that Maria introduced Julia to the person who killed her. How are the family's finances?"

"Didn't ask," I said, wondering how heartless Dahl would have accused me of being if I had. But that was the difference between being a reporter and a private investigator like Rhea.

"It was sex or money," she said, pulling onto the freeway. "Either she was cheating or doing something on the side to get extra money. That's my take. Either way, the friend knows and is afraid of the man."

Such a quick assessment from anyone else based on so little information would have been laughable. But Rhea didn't make seven figures working for elite clientele by being wrong all the time.

"Man?" I repeated, and she nodded.

"Definitely."

At last it hit me, and I laughed. Rhea may be good, but her speculation was always based on fact. "You went to the crime scene, didn't you?"

She smirked as she brought us up to freeway speed and

shooting over to the carpool lane.

"I hate you!" I called over the roar of her engine and the whip of wind.

"I'm sure you'll find a way to live with that," she said back, and we both gave up on talking for a while as we made the forty-minute drive to open land.

Utah. I wanted to hate it. Never in a thousand years would I have ever thought I would be in the Beehive State for anything more than the Sundance Film Festival. It killed me to confess that there were actual perks to living in Mormonville for anyone who was an outdoor enthusiast. It had a mini-city, an international airport, and every type of terrain you could ask for, except for a beach.

My pulse never failed to quicken when residential homes gave way to white fences as we approached the Oquirrh mountains. And a few miles later, those same fences opened to the dirt driveway that led to the pastures that housed my gorgeous palomino, Lady, and Rhea's new Arabian, Hermes.

Being the smart mare she was, Lady recognized Rhea's engine and paced us as Rhea slowed to turn into the drive. Without a word from me, Rhea stopped the second we were off the road.

"See you at the stables," she said, checking her rearview mirror for something besides dust.

"Thanks," I said and leapt from the car, loving that Lady gave a huff of excitement as I hopped the fence. We met in our customary greeting, with her head over my shoulder in a kind of horsy-hug.

"Hey, girl," I cooed, my drawl sneaking out as I spoke to her. "Did you miss me?"

She snorted, which I, of course, took as a yes as I pulled back to look her over.

"I missed you, baby girl. It feels like it's been longer than three days since I last saw you." I stroked her neck as I spoke and checked for signs of dehydration. "It's been hot for October, and I've been worried about you. Are they taking care of you out here?"

She snorted again, which I hoped was another yes. "C'mon," I said, stepping away. "Let's go for a ride."

Knowing those words were all the permission I needed, I gripped her mane and swung onto her bare back, barely touching down before we broke into a full canter toward the pasture gate.

Rhea had already parked and leaned against the fence as we approached. Her naturally bronze skin glowed around those iceberg eyes while her dark hair flowed down her back in a loose braid. What I liked the most, however, was that for one brief moment I didn't see worry lines in her brow as she unlatched the gate and opened it wide enough for Lady to rush through.

"Someone's happy to see you," she observed, allowing Lady to sniff her once we'd circled around.

I slid off and gave Lady a pat. "I've missed her too."

Lady gave me a solid nudge with her nose, obviously dismayed that I had dismounted. Rhea understood the signal as well as I did and smiled.

"I'm with her," Rhea said. "Let's grab Hermes and hit the trail."

Rhea's three-year-old colt, an onyx-black Arabian, was kept in a private pasture next to the geldings and was as easy to spot in a herd of browns as Lady was. One of my neighbors back home bred Arabians. It hadn't been Rhea's plan to buy a horse when we'd picked up Lady, but she and the colt had bonded at first sight. He was a proud horse, and Rhea was a person who understood that pride in an animal should be harnessed, not broken. It was a match made in heaven, which even the owner saw, because he let Hermes go as long as Rhea promised to keep him intact for future breeding. A few hours and a wire transfer later, Hermes and Lady were trailer mates for a cross-country drive. Rhea had ridden him every day since.

"I want to do vaulting," she announced, grabbing his bridle.

"Of course you do," I laughed. "Never mind that you've only been riding for two weeks."

She flashed me one of her trademark smiles. "I was watching it on YouTube. I think I'd be good."

"No question," I agreed. "When are you going to sign up for classes?"

She hesitated. "Well, I was thinking you could teach me."

"I—"

"You have won a lot of trophies and awards in the event," she said over me. "Your neighbor told me."

"Well, wasn't that just neighborly of him," I grumbled.

"Think about it?" she asked, walking over to Hermes.

"Yeah, I'll think about it," I agreed, but really there was nothing to think about. I owed the girl my life. I wasn't going to refuse her anything. That didn't mean I couldn't barter though.

"How about a trade?" I called after her. "I show you vaulting basics and you get me into a certain crime scene."

"Done," she called back and ducked through the fence into Hermes' pasture.

FOUR

I'D BEEN IN *Los Angeles a week, and what did I have to show for it? No job, no new friends, crappy clothes, a roommate obsessed with getting a boyfriend, and a class schedule fit for a half-literate idiot. Technically they were called prerequisites, but I considered them highway robbery.*

Things were not going as I imagined they would. Not by a long shot.

Parking my rear in the same seat I'd occupied the first day of class, I sulked while my fellow investigative journalism students paraded in. The first few days I'd been blinded by their beauty, but now? I'd rather shovel out a horse stall than smell Britney's new perfume again or meet another guy with better hair than mine.

So many times I wanted to call home and tell my brothers what I was seeing. They'd laugh with me, call it all ridiculous, and tell me not to let it bother me. Mama had made me leave my cell phone home, though, and the dorm phones charged for long distance. Until I got a job, I needed to be stingy about where my money went.

The girl with the Chihuahua and her BFF passed again. I hoped the dog crapped in her purse. It was one thing to kill an animal before wearing it, but to accessorize the poor thing while it was alive? Seemed like that should be a crime somehow. A guy I had thought was a girl the first day of class came in wearing short shorts and a midriff. According to my roommate, I was supposed to call the guy 'she' even though he was a he because he'd been born into the wrong body.

That was something I'd maybe forgo in sharing with my brothers. Guys who thought God screwed up? The conversation would be over right there. The. End. God didn't make mistakes. Ever. We'd all met gay people on the rodeo circuit. It wasn't like we were naïve about stuff like that, but there was a difference between saying you were gay and saying God had a senior moment.

Yet as disillusioned as I was, I found myself watching the door for one particular bad boy. Ben Stone definitely didn't think that God had screwed up when he made him a man. No way. And when he walked in wearing a sleeveless shirt and glistening like he just stepped out of the shower, I tried not to look. But in a world where everything was perfect and manicured, Ben Stone was deliciously imperfect. His hair wasn't painstakingly styled. He just let the damp locks fall where they liked and let his natural curl do the styling. The scruff on his jaw added dimension, and his clothes looked lived in, despite their polish.

And Lord have mercy, the boy had a body . . . and a tattoo on his left deltoid, it seemed. I couldn't quite tell what it was a picture of except that it was a star shape with five points. And because his girlfriend had traded in her tank for a toga-style top, I could see the perfect match to his tattoo on her right shoulder.

Twin tattoos? That was serious. Clearly Ben Stone was for display purposes only. Because other girls in the class were looking, just like I was. His girlfriend knew it too. She didn't look at any one of us as she took her seat, but she knew exactly where I was and how I was looking at her man.

Not that I had a shot at him without a corset and a ball gown. I wasn't that delusional, but some of the other girls in the class eyed him like they might take a shot. Rhea ignored them all, just like

I always did whenever girls checked out Jake. Then again, Jake and I didn't have matching tattoos, so there was no reason for me to be territorial. But I'd given Rhea Jensen a little thought since the last class and realized something. She and I were very similar. Back home, I spent all my time with my brothers and their friends. We travelled in a pod, just like Rhea did with those four guys surrounding her.

If she came to the South, I'd be in her shoes and she'd be in mine. The difference being that Southern boys were gentlemen, and no one would give her a dirty look. At least not to her face. We'd get to know a little bit about her before we circled our wagons and left her out in the cold.

"Take your seats," the teacher said as he moved to stand on the floor level in front of the stage. "And sit in groups. Four to six in each group with no more than ten groups total."

Without so much as glancing at us, the professor turned and started setting up papers on the stage.

Seriously? On the second day of class he was forcing us into group work? And just my luck, the nearest person sat four rows ahead of me and chose not to look behind him in a quest for a team. The other students grumbled a bit, but groups were fast forming even as I sat where I was without making a sound. I scanned the auditorium looking for any group with less than four. Against all odds, there wasn't even one, which meant I needed to choose one of the groups and assert myself.

Things like that shouldn't be demeaning, and yet somehow they always are.

Reaching for my bag, I eliminated the Chihuahua group right off the bat. I'd fly solo before I sat next to a purse with incisors. The guy who was a girl might not be a bad choice because then I could find out for sure if he really wanted to be called a "she." I shouldered my pack, still debating, when Rhea stood from her third-row seat and faced the back of the room. I was the only one back there so it was pretty obvious she was looking at me. Her gaze was direct as she indicated the empty seat next to her friend with the shaved head and sat down again.

She'd just invited me to join her group.

As much as that should have made me feel better, I found myself terrified as I moved toward the front of the room. Why had she asked me? What did she want? Was I walking into some unforeseeable trap never to return? Based on the look the girl with the Chihuahua gave me as I headed across the third row to where Rhea sat, that just might be the case. It was hard not to notice her and her friend watching me in pure confusion as I closed the gap between me and Ben.

"Hi," I said, offering a little wave. "Thanks for inviting me to join you."

Rhea face stayed indifferent as Ben smiled from ear to ear. "Well, if that isn't the most adorable accent I've ever heard."

I felt my face flush. "Thank you."

He sent me a playful look that made me blush even more. "Now where is that accent from?"

I'd given up trying to explain to people where I was from. So far I hadn't met a single one who knew Tennessee from Kansas. "The South."

"Alabama," Rhea corrected quickly, and Ben didn't even seem to notice that it was odd she already knew where I was from, but I did.

"Nice," he breathed. "Well, welcome to our group."

"I'm Aaron," the blond one said, raising his hand.

The guy with the shaved head did the same, the tattoo on his upper deltoid catching my eye. "Isaac."

"Danny," said the last, but I was still looking at Isaac's tattoo. It was the same one Ben had and in the same spot.

"Do y'all have the same tattoo?" I asked before I even knew the words left my mouth.

"Yeah," Danny said. "It's the symbol for our band, Pentagram." Isaac and Aaron nodded while Ben looked me over as if he found *something about me confusing. Next to him, Rhea covertly eyed my belt buckle with a look I didn't understand yet.*

"Band? Well, that's nice," I said, hating the amused look Ben sent me every time I opened my mouth. I'd seen it a lot in the past week. Every job interview I'd gone to, every person I'd greeted all looked at me as if they were trying not to laugh. Worse still, they started talking slower and enunciating more, as if they thought I was too dim-witted to understand a conversation at full speed.

"You should come to our next gig," Ben said.

"Sure!" I agreed, maybe a bit too eagerly. Then I remembered I didn't have any money at the moment. "How much are tickets?"

Ben's eyes were glued to my lips. "For you? Free."

Isaac and Aaron shared knowing looks that had me looking at Rhea, who was nodding.

"Yeah, just let us know, and we'll get you in."

Okay, if Rhea wasn't annoyed, maybe Ben wasn't hitting on me. It sure did feel like it, though.

"That's real sweet. I can't wait until I get a job so money won't be quite the issue."

Ben looked me over again. "What kind of job are you looking for?"

"Oh, anything!" I said, knowing my desperation was showing. "I haven't had any luck on campus, and all the stores seem to be staffed just fine. I know they're hiring graveyard cleaners on campus, but I'm really hoping I can find something else."

"Oh, you can definitely do better than that," Ben said, shooting a look to Rhea. "What do you think?"

Her head bobbed. "Gotta use that accent and those legs," she said, as if I wasn't actually in the room. "She'd make a killing in sales."

"I've never had a job," I confessed. "At least not the kind y'all have out here in shops and such."

Rhea's eyes moved over my body like mine would over an auction horse. "You know what couture is?" she asked.

I shook my head.

"Gucci?" she tried again.

The blank look on my face must have sufficed as an answer.

"Cosmetics," she decided, looking at Isaac for agreement. "Imre would train her."

"Definitely," Isaac agreed. "And I can fix her hair up and give her a quick makeover before they meet. I'd love to get my hands on that hair."

I heard the words but was confused as to whether they were still really talking about me.

Rhea seemed to catch on to my confusion. "Isaac's mom is a stylist for Joico. He knows what he's doing."

Her clarification didn't help too much. "Joico?" I echoed.

"Hair color," Ben said. "Isaac does hair for his job."

Now I was totally confused. A boy doing women's hair? "But he doesn't even have any hair himself," I pointed out.

All the guys laughed, and I was quite certain they were laughing at me, not with me.

"He knows enough about hair to know he looks better without it," Rhea said, pointing to her long, shimmering hair. "Isaac styles mine. He's good. You should let him loose on you."

"No charge," he said quickly. "No excuses. I'd just love to show you what I can do with those locks."

I opened my mouth to respond when our teacher chose to interrupt.

"I see everyone has their groups," he said from the front of the class. I quickly dropped into the nearest seat—which just so happened to be next to Ben—as our teacher continued. "Now you won't be working directly with these people for your assignment, but everyone in your group will be given the same situation at the end of class, and when we meet a week from today, we're going to see the different reactions you all had."

Okay, not exactly the assignment I was looking for now that I actually had a group, but it could be worse.

"You'll pick up your assignment on the way out of class, but today," he held up the large stack of stapled papers he'd been arranging on the stage while we all talked. *"You all get the honor of taking a personality quiz that will show your aptitude for the journalism industry."* A few groans erupted around the room.

"Seriously?" Ben said next to me. *"A test the second day of class? Harsh."*

I nodded my agreement.

"No lecture today. No reading assignment," the teacher said over the groans. *"And this test is not based on your reading materials. In fact, if you take this test seriously, it will tell you exactly what field of study would be both the most compatible and fulfilling for you and has been provided to us free of charge by next Tuesday's guest speaker."*

A quick glance around showed that most of the students were less than thrilled.

"So now that I've gotten you all together, I need you to spread out again," he said, indicating the room of mostly empty seats. *"Sit every other row with at least two seats between you and your neighbor."*

"Seriously?" Chihuahua girl objected.

"Seriously," he agreed. *"Now chop-chop."*

* * *

A few porch lights glowed on the Hernandez's street, but it was still as midnight approached. Tuesday nights weren't known for their wild parties, and I thanked the fates for that.

"Thanks again for this," I whispered to Rhea.

"No biggie," she said, fishing her lock-picking kit out of her Bat-bracelet. I'd called the multi-functional accessory many things over the years. Go-Go Gadget Band, Ninja Bracelet, the Bitty Bruce Lee . . . I knew the thing was useful in a pinch, but it still astounded me just how handy it was.

Rhea pointed to the contents of my hands before turning

to the door. "Get your gloves and booties on, and hold the flashlight for me."

I did as she asked, noting something was off with her. When she'd dropped me off after riding she hadn't seemed stressed. She did now, though. She hadn't smiled once since I picked her up, and it was making me feel guilty. In the six months she'd been a Mormon, she'd been trying to be ethical. Was she not comfortable breaking into places anymore?

"Rhea, is everything okay? You seem bothered."

She didn't answer for a moment and focused on the lock instead. "It's not you. Don't worry about it."

If it wasn't me furrowing her brow, then it was Ty. In the past month, the two of them had redefined the term "roller coaster relationship." Rhea loved Ty and Ty loved Rhea. Ty had even proposed to Rhea, but the massive rock he'd purchased for her only made random appearances on her finger. Rhea had some serious life choices to make—as in life or death choices. It's what happened when you unknowingly worked for a bad, bad secret organization who decided they didn't want to let you go.

In a twisted mind game, the man who considered Rhea his property had given her six months to defy her psychological profiling and get married or else work for him until the day she died. If she didn't get married and didn't report for duty in six months, Ty died. If she did get married in that time frame, she'd be offered a final task to buy her way out and repay 'The Fours' for their investment in her. Whatever they asked, it would almost certainly be illegal and likely get her killed.

Or she could leave things as they were, forget about romantic relationships, and just keep working for Mr. Bad for big money.

It was enough to make anyone's brow furrow.

"Listening is what friends do, Rhea. What's up?"

Her hands stopped working on the lock, and she turned to

look at me. "Ty brought up babies again."

I rolled my eyes. That guy seriously needed to practice his Rhea conversations with me more often. "Don't Mormons have to get married first?"

I was glad to see the smile on her lips actually reach her eyes for a split second, but they turned worried again. She looked away.

"He still thinks it's the right move to get married, but I don't think he gets it, Kay. When March rolls around, I'm going to have to do something pretty intense for The Fours. Dying is a possibility, and so is jail time."

That would make me think twice about marrying someone. "What does he say to that?"

She shook her head. "That he's with me no matter what, and he'll take me any way he can have me."

"Good answer," I said, giving Ty a mental high five.

"No. It's a romantic answer," she corrected, turning her attention back to the lock. "He's not thinking straight. We've only known each other six months, Kay, and this isn't a movie. It's very likely things will end very badly."

I disagreed on one point. Ty wasn't the type of guy to surround himself with delusions. He lived very much in reality, and if he said he wanted her, it was because it was true. But she was right about how little he knew. The answer to that was simple, though: fill him in. "Why is he bringing up kids when marriage isn't even on the table?"

She sighed, her hands stopping again. "He says we have the love and the money, so why wait?" The way she paused let me know there was something else, so I waited for her to finish. "He also thinks The Fours will go easier on me if I'm pregnant."

"Oh, Ty," I groaned. Of all the thoughtless and ridiculous things to tell a woman. "How long had you two been arguing before he played that card?"

"A while," she admitted.

"He didn't mean it," I said, touching her arm. "Trust me on this one. He just doesn't want to lose you after everything shakes out in March. We all know you're a runner, and I'm betting he just doesn't want you to skip out on him once you're wallowing in guilt. If you were pregnant, your sense of fair play would bring you back to him. Without that bond, though, you might decide he's better off without your baggage and bolt."

She looked down to her hands. "He is better off without me. So are his kids. Look around, Kay. We're having this conversation while breaking into a residential home. I mean, if there's any evidence I shouldn't be a mother, isn't this it?"

I snickered. "I can't deny that any kid of yours is going to have outright hellion potential."

She turned back to the lock, a smile in her eyes. "I'd be proud of any kid who could outsmart me."

Before I could tell her to watch out what she wished for, there was a click, and the lock released.

"Entrée vous!" Rhea said, pushing the door open. Booties and gloves on, we both entered into a small laundry room adjacent to the kitchen. The place smelled like rotting lettuce.

"Nice," I said through a small gag. "Should have brought masks too."

Rhea nodded. "Let's stick to high traffic areas. They already took the only computer in the house, so we're stuck with the riffraff." She handed me a pocket camera about the size of my pinky and a flashlight. "Document anything of interest and leave everything just as you found it."

"Got it." My voice sounded calm, but my hands shook the slightest bit from adrenaline. It had been a long time since I had broken into someone's house. Okay, I'd never broken into anyone's house, but I didn't want to start acting like a tourist about it. Still, it all seemed incredibly cool until we moved through the kitchen and I caught my first glimpse of blood spatter on the living room wall. Rhea spotted it a split second before I did but not in time to step in front of my flashlight and block my view.

"We won't go in that room. There's too much potential that we'll contaminate evidence." Her voice was clinical and just hard enough to snap me out of the trance the blood had put me in. This was real. I knew that before walking in the door, but seeing it? I didn't feel so well. I'd seen plenty of blood in my day, but this time it struck closer to home.

Yellow tape stretched across the entry opening to the living room. As I moved closer, the nauseating aroma of rotting lettuce was replaced by the tangy smell of blood. It was fourteen hours old, and I could still smell it. Wondering how that was possible, I shined my light into the living room. I saw twice what I would have expected, all soaked into freshly vacuumed carpet. Off to the side, an upright vacuum was still plugged in, as if Julia had just finished.

And Dahl thought this was a suicide? Why would a woman vacuum right before pulling a trigger?

"This way," Rhea said, her arm gently hooking into mine and pulling. My feet didn't want to move. "We're here for motive. That's all. We want to look at any and all papers she may have had. Since this clearly wasn't a suicide, it's likely that some trace of what she was killed for is still here in the house."

"Yeah," I agreed as I swallowed the metallic taste in my mouth and remembered to breathe. I had to keep my game face on. I was a reporter. It was my job to report the news, not personalize it. Unbiased. Uninvested. Getting lost in a wash of emotions didn't help anyone. Finding facts did.

"What are we looking for?" I asked as I flashed my light back into the tidy kitchen. Where was that lettuce smell coming from?

"Anything that catches your eye," Rhea said, moving for the trash can only to realize that it had already been claimed.

"I'll start in her room and see if anything is left in the home office."

"She had an office?"

Rhea didn't meet my eyes, which could mean any number of a million things. "It's a small house. See if you can find any family albums, journals, or anything else that helps start painting a picture."

She didn't need to ask me twice. I nodded and watched her disappear down the hall.

FIVE

*A***FTER TWO HOURS** *with Isaac, I didn't recognize myself. My newly conditioned hair lay flat and smooth, framing my face with an impossible shade of blonde as gorgeous as it was artificial. When I walked out the door with Rhea, I felt sure people on the street would point and laugh.*

"Perfect, Isaac," Rhea said, holding out her hand to motion that I should follow her. "Deja will be doing your makeover, and she is fabulous."

The salon was more than I imagined it would be: tall mirrors, tons of little fancy light bulbs, and sleek images depicting extreme hairstyles on the walls. All the employees were as tall as me, dressed in black, and skinny as rails. And they were all beautiful. This place was expensive—way expensive.

I stopped mid-step, earning a curious look from Rhea's frosty eyes. She pointed down the main hall. "It's just down here."

"I can't accept this," I said, still standing stupidly in the giant bib Isaac had put on me. "It's just too . . . much."

She shrugged my objection off like a fly. "I have money. Besides, I want to do this."

"Why?" It was a reasonable question. "You don't even know me."

A slow smile curved her mouth, one of the few recognizable expressions I'd seen from her at all. "Let's just say you remind me of someone."

"Really? Who?"

She waved the question off. "Doesn't matter. But let's just say she'd be happy to know someone was helping you out, so let's go."

Resistance really was futile since I really did want to see what I would look like once I was done up like all the people around me. And an hour later, when Rhea and Deja walked me up to a full-size mirror, my mouth hung open.

"You'll look even better if you smile," Rhea teased.

But I couldn't. I was too shocked. "Did you give me a face transplant?"

"No," Deja said with her little French accent. "We just accentuated the positive."

The positive? I looked . . . I looked . . . well, if I did say so myself, I looked absolutely fabulous!

"Do you want me to make a package of each the products used today?" Deja asked.

"Yes," Rhea said.

"No!" I objected at the same time, but Rhea won out, and Deja went off to make the package.

"Please, Kay, do you think you can go back to normal after this? With that hair, you've got to have the make-up. It's just how it is."

Kay. No one had called me that before. And I kind of liked it—especially the way Rhea said it. Like we were already friends.

"But I don't know how to put it on," I said.

"Imre will teach you once you're hired, and I'll show you enough to make it until then." She gripped my hands and held their coarseness up next to my newly perfected face. "Now you just need a manicure and a pedicure, and then we'll call it a day, okay?"

I was forced to nod. She was totally right. I couldn't walk around with my rough hands and a refined face. Even I could see that they needed to match, although I couldn't imagine how that was possible. It must be, though, because the skin on my face looked smoother than porcelain, and my eyes had become a shade of blue I'd never imagined when combined with my lightened hair and eye make-up. I looked from my reflection to Rhea, and then back again. It was as if she read my thoughts.

"Yes, you're hotter than me," she said without even a trace of jealousy. "Do you want to gloat about it, or do you want a manicure?"

* * *

My phone rang a few short hours after Rhea and I had called it a night. My eyes peered open and I groaned when I saw the clock read 5:30. I'd only been in bed for three hours.

"What?" I grumbled into my phone.

"Kathryn, it's Nick." He sounded out of breath, but I couldn't make myself care.

"Nick, it's 5:30. Why are you calling me?"

"The Hernandez story," he said, catching his breath. "I'm watching it on the morning news. Their house is on fire!"

I shot up in bed. "On fire? Are you sure?"

"It's a friggin' inferno. Nothing's going to be left of it by the time it's done. Reports say they're only interested in containment at this point."

I grasped around for my remote, finally found it, and turned the television on. My station was on a commercial, so I changed to a rival channel. There it was, just as Nick described—towering inferno destined to be nothing more than rubble by the time it ran its course. I swore under my breath.

"I just thought you'd want to know."

"Good call, Nick. Thanks." I hung up on him, staring at the TV as guilt washed over me. Had Rhea and I somehow started the fire? Was it my fault?

Having no choice, I hit my speed dial and prayed Rhea

would forgive me for waking her up.

"You saw it?" she said after the first ring.

"The fire? Yeah, you?"

"I'm looking at it right now," she replied. "It wasn't us, Kay. The fire hasn't been going too long, and the rear kitchen window is smashed in. Two other windows in the house are smashed in the same way. It's arson."

"Are you there?" I asked in awe.

"Yeah. Ty wanted me to show him where we were last night, so we passed by on our running route. I stopped when I saw the smoke, but he had to head home to get to work."

"Where are you exactly?" I asked, feeling like I should do something. Anything. I should definitely be there reporting, but by the time I got there, the blaze would be out. I turned the TV back to my station to see who was reporting.

"In a neighbor's tree between the property line in the back yard," Rhea said.

I digested that, realizing she was at most fifty feet from the blazing fire. She had to be feeling it. "How do you know the firemen didn't break the windows?"

"Because I got here before them. Besides, the fire department is focusing on ventilating the roof, not busting small windows."

"Anyone there from my station?"

"Yeah, Tanya. She's down the street a little ways."

"I need to get into work before someone else poaches this out from under me."

"Kay?" she said before I could hang up.

"Yeah."

"Talk to the friend. You'll have to lean on her hard. Whoever did this didn't just want to burn potential evidence. It doubles as a scare tactic to those who know who he is. Like Maria. If he doesn't go down fast, someone else could die."

I took a deep breath, imagining all the hierarchal red tape

in the way of making that happen. "I'll need everything—and I mean everything—you can dig up on Julia."

"I'm headed home now."

"Okay. Talk to you later." It was going to be a messy day.

SIX

*R*HEA CLAIMED SHE *had some jewelry that would be just perfect for me, and since she was driving, my objections to dropping by her house didn't carry much weight. When we arrived, I thought we'd pulled up to a country club that smelled like heaven. The whole yard was acre after acre of perfection. Every bloom flawless, every tree trimmed back, and bushes you could take a plumber's line to.*

"You live here?" I gawked.

"Mm-hmm," she said, going half way through the roundabout adjoining the front steps and parking. "This'll just take a second. Come on in."

I had the distinct impression that the soil in Rhea's yard was cleaner than my boots, which had me hesitating as I exited her convertible. The cobblestone beneath my feet definitely was, and the windows nearly blinded me as I watched Rhea move to her front door.

"This place is amazing!" I said.

"Yeah," she agreed. "More than any two people need, for sure."

"Two?" I asked, thinking the number sounded low.

"Me and my dad," she said. "And this doubles as his office. He's a landscape architect."

"No kidding," I breathed, following her into the lobby. The

huge entrance extended up three stories and stretched the width of the house, with an exit straight to the back. On either side were massive staircases leading up with arches underneath them leading to the main level of the house.

"Whoa."

"Come on up," she said, motioning to the stairs on the right.

I followed her up the massive marble staircase to the second floor hallway. It felt sinful to be wearing my boots on the Persian rugs, but Rhea didn't say anything. After yards and yards of hallway, Rhea turned left into what I assumed was her bedroom. Either that, or a princess lived there.

"Holy cow," was all I could say as my eyes drank in the four-poster bed, lush carpet, and large oil paintings around her room. Centered at the base of her bed was a gorgeous statue with four angels. Unable to stop myself, I stepped forward and touched it. "Did you make this?"

She laughed outright. "Hardly. It's a replica of the Four Freedoms by Walter Russell."

"It's gorgeous," I breathed.

"I think so too."

I wanted to ask about the paintings too, but didn't want to come across as a total hick, so I refrained.

"I've got some great bracelets that I never wear," she said walking up to an old fashioned vanity. "And a necklace I know Imre will love."

She made it all seem normal, like she lent fine jewelry out to strangers every day. I wanted to say something, but what? Rhea didn't listen to objections and brushed off thanks. Biting my lip and trying to figure out how I could ever repay her, I drew close to see what she was picking out for me and caught sight of a picture. The woman looked just like Rhea, only a bit older and with sea green eyes. The woman's hair and skin were distinctly ethnic, and Rhea looked just like her—just a few shades lighter. Her dad was probably white, although I didn't see any pictures of him in her room.

"That your mom?" I asked, and for a brief moment Rhea's hands stilled. Yes, it was her mom. And one thing was for sure, her mother didn't live with her anymore. "She's beautiful."

"She was," Rhea agreed, confirming my suspicion. Rhea's mom had died.

We were both looking at the photo now, and I sensed that Rhea had spent hours studying it just as she was in that moment.

"She died in her sleep when I was a kid," she said in response to my unasked question. "Doctors said it was a stroke."

"I'm so sorry." Mama and I may not currently be on good terms, but at least I still had her.

"Yeah," Rhea said as she got back to searching through her jewelry. "Her family disowned and disinherited her when she came to America for an education, but she did it anyway."

Her words hung in the air between us, and I wondered if she could possibly know she was describing me and my situation.

"Got it," she said, pulling out a gold chain with an elaborate tree pendant. "He'll love this. You can wear it with what you're wearing now, but the bracelets will have to wait until you've upgraded a bit." A little beaded bag appeared out of nowhere and she placed her jewelry in it. My attention was still on the hauntingly beautiful woman in the picture.

"I look nothing like her," I said, knowing she would understand the reference.

"No. You don't."

I bit my lip before realizing I was now wearing lipstick. "But is she the one I remind you of? Are you helping me because of her?"

Rhea's hand faltered in handing me the bag, and I watched her debate her answer. "My mom came to Los Angeles from Persia without knowing a single soul." She glanced at the photo again. "Imagine a woman that beautiful being dropped off in the middle of Hollywood. She was so naïve that this place nearly ate her alive. And it would have if someone with influence hadn't helped her." She sent me an uncomfortable look. "We're not nice here, Kay.

That's the first thing you have to learn. 'Nice' will get you stabbed in the back so hard that you may never breathe right again."

"But you're being nice to me," I objected.

"No. I'm doing this to honor my mom. It's selfish."

I didn't believe her for a second, but it seemed important to her that I did. "Okay."

She wasn't done. "The boys will want to use you, and the girls are going to do anything they can to make you ugly. You have to trust me on this and really question anyone who's being nice to you because they want something."

"Okay," I drawled, trying not to be amused by her intensity. I knew a thing or two about social tactics. I hadn't grown up in a cave. Just Alabama.

Her eyes narrowed, as if debating whether or not to say more, but then she just handed me the bag. "You should see the view off my balcony before we leave. It's awesome."

"I'd love to," I said, happy for a change in subject.

She headed to the large double doors as I brought up the rear. I was only a few steps from the balcony door when a paper on her desk caught my attention. There was a Greek symbol in the header, and after reading the first line, I realized Rhea had been invited to pledge a sorority.

If I had stayed in the South, I would be getting letters too. Coming from a line of gin makers meant something in the South but not in Hollywood.

Feeling deflated, I joined Rhea on her balcony and immediately caught my breath. "Sweet heaven!"

Her backyard was more garden than yard, with everything oriented around a Vegas-worthy fountain that was shooting water thirty feet into the air. Around the fountain were a series of massive hedges that surely appeared like a maze on ground level, but from Rhea's balcony it looked like an ancient coin.

"You wake up to this every morning?" I asked in awe.

She nodded. "I never get used to it."

I bit my lip again, fighting a wave of self-pity. "I could never live in a place like this."

For the first time Rhea looked like she disapproved of me, but the look was short lived. "Life gives you exactly what you ask for, Kay. You will live in exactly the kind of house you picture for yourself, whether it's a mansion or a hut."

I looked at Rhea then, right into those sharp eyes of hers, and believed her. It made absolutely no sense to do so, but I did. My eyes flicked back to where the letter of invitation sat on Rhea's desk.

"Does that go for everything?" I asked.

She nodded. "Everything."

I closed my eyes for a brief moment and imagined who I would be if she was right.

* * *

Arriving an hour early, I found Carla, my manager, fielding calls in her office. Two words best described Carla: Ann Taylor. There was an outlet store up in Park City, and I was pretty sure Carla shopped there exclusively. Both conservative and unimaginative, Carla's wardrobe was the first indicator of how she chose to approach the news: predictably and without flare. Needless to say, we were having a hard time warming up to each other.

I watched her for a moment, preparing myself for everything I knew she'd say before catching her when she finally had a break between calls.

"It's been non-stop since five this morning, I swear," she said with a groan.

"Well, it's your lucky day, then, because there isn't a reporter out there who knows more about the Hernandez story than I do. It's mine."

Carla shook her head. "Can't do that, Kathryn. I know you introduced viewers to this yesterday, but it's Angela's now."

I arched a brow at her. "And what qualifies her to do this

story beyond that fact that she hasn't even shown up for work yet?"

"She'll replace Tanya at the scene at nine. It's already been decided."

I'd known this would be the case. Angela had clout while I was a fresh face. "You realize this is favoritism, right?"

She shot me a glare. "Watch yourself. You've been here five weeks, Kathryn. Angela's been here eight years. Utah knows her." And likes her. She didn't say it, but she didn't have to.

"That doesn't mean she can walk onto the scene, state the obvious, and call it news," I shot back. "Does she know how many kids Maria had and who has them? Does she know her sister's name, the criminal histories involved here, or how the fire started? Does she have sources who will tell her things off the record that will turn out to be true when every other station reports them a week later?" True, I had none of these things yet, but I would.

Fingers threaded through her hair, Carla stared at her desk.

"You know Angela will just say whatever you spoon feed her," I pressed. "She's a good reporter, but she's going in blind. I'm not."

It was probably the first time all day Carla was glad to have her phone ring. "Out of my hands," she said and dismissed me with a flick of one hand as she picked up the phone with the other.

Did she think it was that easy to brush me off? Had she forgotten she worked with reporters? I shook my head and made sure I spoke loud enough that she couldn't help but hear me. "No, it's not, Carla. Make it happen."

I didn't give her a chance to reply as I walked out of her office and called Nick.

"Where are you?" I snapped when he picked up.

"Picking up a caffeinated beverage to make sure a certain someone doesn't bite my head off."

Despite my anger, I smiled. "You're not on scene?"

"Nope. I bailed when I heard Angela was coming in." He paused, and I heard the ambient noise of the coffee shop in the background. Like most Mormons, the guy didn't even drink coffee, and yet he'd started bringing it in for me every morning. Apparently Mormons didn't go to hell for being the middle man. "Sorry you lost the story, Kathryn."

For a moment I was disgusted. "Have I taught you nothing?"

"Uh, no?"

I almost laughed. "We're poaching it back, idiot."

There was a stunned silence and then a resigned sigh. "Of course we are."

"Get your butt in here," I said and hung up.

SEVEN

THE MAN STANDING on the stage with our investigative journalism teacher sure did look impressed with himself. The flawless suit and shiny shoes he wore probably cost a bundle. I was aware of it because he was aware of it. He smiled a lot and liked to pat our teacher on the shoulder like I would pat a dog.

If my teacher realized he was being patronized, he didn't show it. He clapped his hands and called us to order as I took the empty seat next to Ben again. Chihuahua girl and her sidekick sent me death stares.

"Take your seats, everyone!" he called out. "We aren't going to waste a minute of class today because we have a rare and honored guest."

No one in the class looked particularly awed, so I assumed the man wasn't famous. If he wasn't famous, he wasn't worthy of emulation. That pretty much seemed to be the attitude.

Gesturing over to the guest, he continued his introduction. "Elliott Church is a private investigator to the rich and famous. Today, he is here to talk to us about the difference between an investigator and a journalist in addition to explaining to each of you the results of your test."

The interest level in the room picked up, and I noted that even Rhea leaned forward in her chair. This man actually interested her.

"Now give a big hand to welcome our guest, Elliott Church."

We all clapped in an obligatory way as Elliott smiled and took center stage. "No, really," he laughed. "Save the clapping for when you actually mean it." A few students laughed, and Rhea's eyes narrowed as I watched her watch him.

"First of all, let me say that the honor is all mine," he began, reaching over to a small stand and picking up our tests to hold up. "There's great potential in this room, and I have the proof right here in my hands. Some of you won't be journalists, but deep down, you already know that. You don't need me to tell you that, but I will. I'll also tell you what you're best suited to do because that's my gift. I see potential and how to best harness it. And that gift has made me obscenely rich."

A few more students were giving him their undivided attention, but I could feel that he still hadn't captured the room's interest until he made his next move.

"But talking is one thing. Before I hand these back to you, I will show you exactly how well I know you by asking questions. Here's how this will work: I'll ask a question and then choose the person in this room best qualified to answer it." He smiled then, as if holding back a secret he wasn't going to share. "So we'll start with Jasmine." Then, weirder than weird, he looked straight at Chihuahua girl. "Who made this suit?"

She was at least fifty feet away. There was no way she could know the answer. At least that's what I thought until Jasmine rolled her eyes and said, "Kiton. You got it in Italy. Same with your shoes."

He nodded that she was correct even as my jaw dropped in shock. "Excellent."

How had she done that? It was only while looking around in wonder that I realized that about half the class could have answered that question and really wasn't all that impressed by Jasmine or Elliott yet.

Elliott's gaze moved to the center of the room to single out a jock. "Brandon, how many girls are in this room?"

"Uh, thirty-seven," he said, earning a chuckle from the class. Elliott laughed right along.

"And Jay, how many chairs?"

I had no idea who Jay was until Rhea looked at the guy in girl's clothes who cleared his throat nervously. "Including on the stage?" he/she asked.

"The whole room," Elliott agreed, without even looking at the stacks of chairs stored behind him.

"Four hundred and twenty seven," Jay said, earning a few grumbles of doubt. Our guest didn't miss them.

"Endo, is Jay right?"

A quiet Asian kid in the front row nodded. "Yes."

"They could just be making that up!" a jock said from toward the back. I didn't know his name, but I was guessing that Elliott did.

"Is that so, Caleb?" he asked. "Tell me, which NFL team has won the most consecutive regular season games?"

He snorted as if the question disgusted him. "Indianapolis Colts. Please, everyone knows that."

"Perhaps," Elliott said, even though I hadn't had a clue. "But the point is that you are the best qualified person in this room to answer that question. Just like Ben is the best qualified to answer this one." He looked straight at Ben sitting next to me, but I noticed that Rhea kept her eyes on our guest, her interest totally captured. "0111001001101000011001011000001. What did I just spell, Ben?"

Was the guy kidding? Or insane? Endo, who had started writing the numbers as Elliott said them looked confused as he stared at the sequence and then turned around to see what Ben would say. Both Rhea and Ben shared a look before she shrugged as if to say, "Well? Answer the guy."

"It spells 'Rhea' in binary code," Ben said, totally stunning me. Endo looked back to his paper with the numbers on it and started *adding little ticks, but still seemed a little confused.*

"R-h-e-a, Endo," Elliott clarified, earning a knowing "ahhh" from the kid. "And Rhea is going to choose who will answer my last question." Once again, he looked straight at Rhea without anyone pointing her out. It was eerie. "Rhea, who would best know what item is missing from this list: juniper berries, coriander seed, angelica root, licorice root, orange peel."

The entire class grew silent as Elliott posed the one question I knew the answer to so far. The problem was, Rhea didn't know that I knew. I wanted to catch her eye and send her a signal but found her already looking at me. "She knows."

Caleb and his buddies actually laughed behind me. "She would know how to bake a pie."

"It's not a pie recipe," I shot back, feeling heat rise to my face at having everyone chuckle at what he said. "They're gin botanicals." Turning back to Elliott, I added, "And I'd put orris root on that list."

"Exactly," Elliott said, but he wasn't looking at me. He was looking at Rhea like a new favorite toy, and she was looking right back. "Now that I've shown you how well this test profiles your strengths, I'm going to hand them back to you. Stapled to the top will be a computer printout of a few jobs that fit your strengths. I recommend exploring those fields, since you will excel with ease."

He passed the pages to our teacher, who appeared from the sidelines to play assistant and handed them all back. I understood his excitement now. Elliott may not be an investigative reporter, but if he chose to be, he would be amazing. And he definitely had us all waiting impatiently to get our packets back. Mine would say I should be a reporter—I knew it. And if it didn't, well, it was only because I hadn't take the test seriously and fudged a bit on the answers.

The room crescendoed in excitement as more and more students got their results. From the sounds of it, people liked what they were seeing. On our row, Ben got his back first and didn't seem to mind when I looked over his shoulder.

"Software programmer?" I asked. I probably would have listed a hundred other occupations before bringing up computers as an option for Ben.

He shrugged. "Software's easy. I've always dabbled." The admission seemed to make him uncomfortable even as Rhea smiled as if they'd had the discussion before.

"Katie?" our teacher said, looking around for me. I raised my hand and eagerly took the papers. Five occupations were listed, and I just knew what number one would be.

"Sociocultural Anthropologist?" I said, my nose scrunching up in distaste. I could barely say it and didn't have the first idea what the words meant, so I scanned down the other professions for the one I was looking for. And there it was, in the number five slot. Investigator. "Yes!" I breathed, showing it to anyone who wanted to look. "See that? Investigative Reporter!"

Okay, so I added the reporter part, but the two went together, right?

"Nice," Rhea said, although she seemed more interested in the rest of my list, which included Charity Organizer, Entrepreneur, and Teacher. I'd never given a thought to any of those professions and wasn't about to start just because a computer printout told me to.

I was going to be a reporter! I was a natural at investigating, according to this fancy test. I would succeed!

"Rhea," my teacher muttered just before coming down our row again and handing her packet across me and Ben. There was no list on her top sheet. Just a two-sentence invitation: You're hired. See me after class if you're interested.

No one said anything when she immediately flipped the packet over face down without seeming to look at it.

"Aren't you going to see what it says?" Aaron asked her.

"No," she said easily as Elliott took command of the stage again. A brief raise of his hand, and the room fell silent.

"Now that we've got that out of the way, let's discuss the difference between an investigator and a journalist and why you must choose between the occupations."

He had the room's full attention. He'd converted a room full of critics in about ten minutes. Including me. Totally impressive.

And my mind was swimming with so much information by the time I left class that I didn't even remember to watch to see if Rhea stayed after to accept Elliott's offer.

* * *

I'd played it over and over in my mind and kept coming up with the same answer. I needed to talk to Dahl. If anyone could be swayed into helping me, it was him. Yes, there were cops who liked me more, but they weren't leaving the force in two weeks. They wouldn't have a sense of urgency to make a difference. And most of all, they'd never seen me in the trenches and witnessed how far I was willing to go to get the bad guy.

If I wanted to know what the police knew, Dahl was the one I needed to apply my charm on. I'd used Bambi eyes on him before and come out on top. If I played things right, I might just be able to reel him in twice.

"Whatever you're thinking about, you look like a serial killer," Nick said between sips of Zrii—one of the billion multi-level-marketing health drinks produced in Utah.

"You've got to think like one to stop one," I justified.

The important thing to remember with Dahl was to appeal to his sense of nobility. If I came on too strong, he'd walk and not look back. Sex wasn't going to be what brought him to my side, which helped me breathe easier. Dahl would help me if I could show him I had what it took to close this case with record speed. I needed to convince him that he needed my skill set and back-door approach to apprehend a killer.

"We're making a detour before the TRAX station story," I told Nick. Carla had been wise to assign the story on a toddler who had fallen off a TRAX platform over the phone so she could avoid being subjected to my death glare. No one had even gotten hurt. She would have to try a whole lot harder to distract me from the Hernandez story.

Nick downed the rest of his drink and tossed the can in my recycle bin. "Figured that."

"We're going to find out what Maria Bernal knows about her friend's death."

"And if she doesn't know anything?"

"She does," I said, leaving no room for argument. "You can stay in the van if you don't want to watch me lean on her."

Nick raised an eyebrow at me. "That's pretty mercenary of you. Her friend hasn't even been dead twenty-four hours."

I shook my head at his cute naiveté. "Think about it, Nick. Your best friend just died. You're the only one who knows what happened, but if you say anything, you'll end up dead too. You want to talk, but you're afraid. All you need is a reason, and the longer you wait, the more you feel the pressure building up in you. She wants to talk. I just have to make it safe for her to do so."

"By intimidating her in her own home and stabbing a hot poker into her shame and guilt until she breaks?" he finished for me, heavy on sarcasm.

"Basically," I agreed.

"Yeah," he said, walking away from my desk. "I'll wait in the van."

J **ASMINE AND CARMINA** *pranced away, yappy dog in tow.*
My hand shook as I held the stationery with a letter they had handed me at the end of class. It was twin to the one I had found on Rhea's desk when I'd visited her house. I'd been chosen. A sorority wanted me. And not just any sorority, an elite one! It was almost enough to make me want to call Mama, disowned or not.

"They want me," I said in reflexive shock to Rhea. "I can pledge your sorority!"

A thrill unlike any I had ever felt before filled me as these words left my mouth, and I thought I might scream with excitement until it registered that Rhea was not smiling. In fact, she looked a little mad. In my elation I tried to convince myself I had imagined seeing this and felt slightly relieved when she smiled and said, "Congratulations."

"Thanks! Yeah . . . I can't believe it!" And I couldn't. Being in a sorority meant that people might actually look at me from here on out. Well, at least girls. Ever since Rhea's makeover and me getting a job at MAC, I'd been getting plenty of looks from the fellas.

"We should celebrate. Let me take you out to dinner," she suggested, though her tone was oddly flat.

"Oh, I couldn't. Besides, I'm not in yet."

"Neither am I," Rhea pointed out, although both of us knew

that was nothing more than a technicality.

"Thank you so much, Rhea!" I said, throwing my arms around her. "I couldn't have done this without you." In truth, I had no idea how I had done it. It made no sense, but I wasn't about to look a gift horse in the mouth.

"Don't thank me," she said, and meant it. "If they want you, it's for their own reasons." She stepped away. "Look, I need to get to my next class, but we'll talk about this later, okay?"

"Yeah. Of course. I've got work, anyway." I tried not to let her distinct lack of enthusiasm be a killjoy. Rhea just never got excited. Ever. Or at least, if she had, I hadn't seen it in the few weeks I'd known her. Calling her cold seemed harsh, but she was definitely a few degrees cooler than I was used to, and I was used to hanging around guys.

"Be careful," she said, and walked away.

Be careful? What kind of ominous farewell was that?

Great. Now I was barely excited anymore. Okay, maybe I still was, but I needed someone to gush with. I walked out of class and onto campus in hopes of catching someone—anyone—and spotted a shaved head.

"Isaac!" I called, racing after him. Thank heavens he heard me the first time and stopped as I hurtled toward him and shoved the envelope at him as soon as he was in range. "I'm in! A sorority is letting me pledge."

"Cool," he said, his voice warm and enthusiastic. "That must be exciting for you."

"Are you going to be in a frat?" I asked.

He shook his head. "Nah, we don't roll that way. Rhea's doing it because her mom was in that sorority, but we boys like to play like we're too cool."

I laughed, loving how easy it was to talk to Isaac. "Well, shoot. Guess I won't see you at the parties then."

"Oh, you'll see us," he corrected. "We're definitely crashers."

I snatched the letter back. "Well, no sense in putting the cart *before the horse. I've got to make it in first."*

"Good luck," he said.

"Okay," I sighed. "I've got to go now. I have another makeup class for my job, but talk to you soon?"

"Totally," he agreed and started off the other way.

Moving back the way I came, my steps slowed as I spotted something I probably wasn't supposed to see. In fact, I was certain I wasn't.

Rhea hadn't rushed off to her next class. She had rushed after Jasmine and Carmina, and based on their body language, Rhea was furious. Jasmine and Carmina, however, didn't look the slightest bit upset. Whatever she'd said to them, Jasmine dismissed it with a wave of her hand and walked away.

Rhea stood there then, both hands in her back pockets and eyes so focused they looked lethal. She'd been talking about me getting an invitation. I knew it. But why was she so mad? The girl usually had such a poker face, but she'd been screaming mad. And I was left wondering why.

* * *

I didn't have as much time as I wanted, but I knocked on Maria's door anyway. A second later a munchkin-sized face peeked out the living room window as a dog did its best to sound vicious. Great. A dog.

The little girl ran away from the window just before the peephole went dark. I waved to let them I know I noticed. "I just want to talk to you for a second, Maria."

"Go away!" she yelled over her snarling dog.

"Not until you talk to me," I said. "And I can stand here all day."

"I'll call the police!"

"Yeah, do that." There was no way she'd call. If Rhea and I were right, the last thing she would want would for the bad guy to hear she'd invited cops to her house. He might think she was cooperating. "Or you can just give me five minutes. You're call."

She chose option C: opening her door and letting her dog loose on me. Like every third dog in Utah, it was a pit bull. I pulled on the door handle to trap the dog between the door and its frame when it was only half way out.

"Seriously?" I yelled at her. "You have a death wish for your dog? If it bites me, they'll put it down."

"He'll get three strikes," she called back, chin high and face arrogant. Was I seriously risking bodily harm to help this woman? Her snarling dog was about two inches from putting a run in my nylons.

"Not a pit bull," I said. "And not when it bites a reporter. Call it off before I hurt it."

Her eyes challenged mine for a moment before she reached through the crack and gripped her dog's collar, yanking it back into the house.

"Thank you," I breathed, letting go of the door and wiping dog spittle off my hem of my Neiman Marcus skirt. Totally gross. And dog saliva never dried well. If I hadn't ruined her day first, I would have sent her a dry cleaning bill. As it was, we were probably even.

Knowing she would come out now, I stood and waited. I didn't have to wait long.

"Why won't you leave?" she hissed, charging out her door and trying to back me down her front steps by her mere presence.

"Tell me," I said, not flinching. "I know you're scared but there has to be something you can tell me that won't be traced back to you. Is there something I can trip over? Someplace I can go to see what I need to see?"

"I don't know what you're talking about!"

I shook my head, keeping my voice low. "We both know that's a lie. We also both know that everyone on your street is watching us right now. That's why you're freaked out. And that's why you tried to sic your dog on me and why you came outside to scream at me. You need people to see you chasing me off, and the longer I stay, the worse your credibility gets."

"And yet you won't leave," she sneered.

"I will as soon as you give me what I need." Man, this sucked. Rhea was so much better at "leaning" than I was. But now that she was trying to prove to a super-secret society that she was out of the investigating game, things like this weren't really up her alley. That she had gotten me into the Hernandez's the night before was a huge risk for her. The bummer was that I didn't even think it was worth it. We hadn't really found much.

"Tell me, Maria." I held up my hands as if she had the upper hand and I was backing down. "As long as this man is free, he's going to threaten you and your family. It won't stop. Help me find him."

She stabbed her finger into my collarbone, fully intending for it to hurt, I'm sure. "Maybe you should worry about your own business and leave other people's families alone!"

I so didn't have time for this. I had to go inform the citizens of Utah that a toddler had fallen off of a TRAX platform and get a statement from UTA even though at the moment I really didn't care.

"One thing," I repeated. "You give me one solid hint, and I tuck my little tail and walk away. Better yet, if it pans out, I won't come back. Ever." This time my words sunk in as she sent nervous looks to her neighbors' homes.

Her finger gouged me again, and her expression kept its disdain even as her words changed and volume dropped. "You need to go now. You have no idea who you're messing with."

"I'm sure I've dealt with worse."

She shook her head with naked disgust. "Your kind doesn't even understand what worse is."

"Okay. If it makes you feel better to think that, sure." The point wasn't worth arguing. "The reality for you, though, is that you're going to keep seeing my face again and again until you tell me something that helps me catch the man who killed your friend."

Maria got up so close to me that I could smell the onions and cilantro on her breath. "She wrote it all down and stuck it in a cave about seven miles up Little Cottonwood. That's all I know. They will come to question me as soon as you leave, and if they hurt my children because you came here, I will shoot you myself. Understand?"

"Completely. Now yell at me or something, and I'll get out of your hair."

It wasn't an act when the stream of shrill Spanish coming from her mouth knocked me back on my heels. Wow, the woman had pipes. I backed away, covering my ears until I took refuge in the van. Still, Maria kept on screaming.

"Happy?" Nick asked, starting the engine. He, at least, was fooled.

"Totally," I said, keeping a smile from my face just in case we really were being watched.

PLEDGING WASN'T AS *bad as the movies made it seem—at least not for my sorority. More than anything, it seemed like my gossip skills were being graded. And it's not like I enjoy gossiping exactly, but I am from the South. Spinning a yarn comes as easy as breathing.*

And since my soon-to-be sorority sisters were trying to talk about something I knew two shakes about, we always seemed to talk about the same subject: Ben Stone.

"They've got to be together," Jasmine was saying. "Katrina basically threw herself at Ben, and he didn't even look at her. Just tossed her to the side and went off to band practice."

"But he and Rhea never kiss," Carmina objected. "At least not that I've ever seen."

"So they're on the down-low. A guy like him has got to be getting it somewhere." Jasmine's eyes narrowed on me and her finger stabbed out my direction. "You hang out with them. What do you think?"

My body tensed in anger. Rhea and I hadn't really talked since I shared the news with her that I was pledging. I didn't talk and she didn't push. Instead, I'd been spending more time with my new sisters.

I shrugged as if I didn't care. "They're joined at the hip, but

I've never seen them do anything."

"Hmph," Jasmine said under her breath, her dark eyes clearly plotting. "I bet you could get Ben, Kay!" Ever since Rhea had called me Kay in class, everyone had started using the nickname. It felt . . . different. Then again, so did I.

"Me?" I choked. I had come quite a way in thinking more highly of myself, but I hadn't reached the point of putting myself on the same level as Rhea—even if she was possibly a traitor who tried to sabotage me from Greek life.

If Rhea was jealous that I had other friends, that was her problem. I couldn't be her special project forever.

"Why not?" Jasmine pressed. "I've seen Ben watch you."

"Uh, I don't think so."

Carmina reached out and stroked my hair. "You should two-tone your hair. You'd look so awesome that way."

"Really?" I said, not even sure what two-toning was, not to mention if I had enough money to pay for it. I thought Isaac had done a great job with my current color. Yet even being the hillbilly everyone thought I was, I could tell that the time was fast approaching for me to cover my roots. I was sure I didn't want to know what that was going to cost me.

Maybe if I started dating Isaac he would do it for free.

The thought hit me before I realized it. It was so catty . . . so . . . Jasmine. Rhea was one of Isaac's best friends, and even she had paid him. Then again, she wasn't kissing the guy, and if I did—

I stopped myself, not sure whether to be pleased or appalled at the direction of my thoughts. Purposefully dating a guy just for the free services? I'd never even considered that before.

"Well, if you're not going for him, I will," Jasmine said with an air of authority.

"Ben?" I asked in shock. "How?"

"At the social this Friday. He'll crash with his crew, and I'll snag him."

I was too shocked to say anything. I was sitting in a room listening to a girl plot to steal Ben away from Rhea. No matter how mad I was at Rhea for trying to block me from becoming her sorority sister, I hadn't quite gotten to the point where I wanted her to lose her boyfriend.

But when I saw Rhea in class the next day, I didn't say a thing. I justified myself by saying that there was no way Jasmine would succeed anyway, but that didn't chase away the awful feeling I had in my stomach.

* * *

Nick and I took footage of the TRAX location, interviewed the mom who "only looked away for a second," and got UTA's statement. After a little editing, it would be a great filler story reminding mothers everywhere to hold on tight to their children when massive trains approached.

As Nick and I headed back to the station, I couldn't help but stare at the mountains. I'd need Google to tell me where I was going, but somewhere up there lay a clue that would lead me to the man who had killed Julia Hernandez. It was time to charm Dahl and get some collaboration going so I could have access to everything that police had taken from her home.

I had to wait until Nick was out of earshot, though. The boy was learning fast, but he was still too innocent for this kind of stuff. Having the conversation in the office was off limits too, I realized as we pulled into the parking garage. I'd need to go off site, somewhere the wrong people wouldn't overhear and talk Dahl into meeting me in person. Hanging up on me was too easy. Plus, I couldn't use my big blues on him over the phone.

The moment the van parked, I was out the door and taking the stairs to the main level. I pushed through the doors and onto the street, dialing the second crisp October air hit my skin.

"Kathryn?" a male voice called behind me. Vaguely recognizing it, I turned and looked. The Brooks Brothers suit and Cordovan cap toes registered first, followed by the man's firm, trim body and lean face.

Alan White. He was a lawyer I'd interviewed a few days back. He'd been a little flirty, and I hadn't fought him on it, since we'd had technical problems and it filled the time.

"Alan," I called back, hitting the end button on my call to Dahl while I got rid of this guy. "How are you?"

"Better now that I've seen you."

Gag. It was time for him to find a new line. "Well, I'm sorry I need to cut out on you. Perhaps we could talk another time?"

"How about Friday night?" he offered without missing a beat. He'd planned on this. "There is a fund raising auction, and I would love to have you accompany me."

"Accompany" him? We both knew what he meant by that, and the answer was "not a chance." "I don't have my calendar with me," I said. "Can I get back to you on that?"

"Of course," he said, his hand reaching out to run down my arm like it had a right to do so.

Ignoring the abrupt tightness in my chest, I took another step away. "I'll get back to you."

He smiled. "I'll look forward to it."

The guy gave me the creeps, even though he was the type of guy I usually dated. A little bit of irony there, but I had other things to worry about. I called Dahl again, relieved when he picked up.

"Hey, Dahl," I said. "Where can we meet?"

"Oh, you know my name this time?" he replied, sounding a little petty.

"Excuse me?"

"Last time you called me Alan."

Whoops. "Different guy. Look, I have info, and I know you have a suspect. I think we can help each other."

He hesitated. "You know I can't talk to you about the case."

"Really, Dahl? Even if it means catching a killer in record time?"

"That's not your job," he said, his voice sounding dark and dangerous. It wasn't fair that he be blessed with both good looks and a good voice. "You're a reporter, Kathryn. You report news. You don't make it."

"Please, if I had a dollar for every time I've heard that," I groaned.

"It's because it's true. If you wanted to be a detective, you should have taken that career path."

"Or I could forget about labels and job titles and just be a human who gets things done. Now are you going to meet me or not?"

"No." There was no flexibility in his tone, which only made it more fun that I was about to make him eat his refusal.

"Fine. I guess you don't care that I'm about to go up unfamiliar mountains in search of something that might prove to implicate your suspect."

Again, a pause. "Who says we have a suspect?"

I laughed, not letting him know I was fishing. "You do. And don't deny it. And also don't pretend that I don't have a friend who can tell me who it is with one phone call."

"That's a bluff," he retorted. "Records are too tight. There's no way Rhea would know."

Bingo. He'd just confirmed that police did, in fact, have a suspect. "You have a lot to learn, Dahl. On the top of that list should be not to underestimate Rhea Jensen."

This time he laughed. "Sorry, but I have a whole lot on my list ahead of that."

We were talking in circles, getting nowhere. "You haven't answered my question, Dahl. You with me on my scavenger hunt? My lead story tonight could be Salt Lake Police arresting a murderer."

"Yeah," he scoffed. "Let's pretend this is about me."

"It could be. Let me know," I said and then hung up. There was no reason to talk to him anymore. It was probably a mistake to talk to him in the first place, but he was my best choice for cooperation. My gut still said that.

Walking back up to the front entrance, the second my foot crossed the threshold, Carla was at my neck.

"My office. Now!"

Crap. "Can I go to the bathroom first?" That threw her.

"Two minutes!" she all but yelled, earning us a few looks in the lobby.

I flashed her an over-friendly smile. "Be right up."

The second I was out of her sight, I called Rhea. It rang . . . and rang . . . and rang. The call was just shy of going to voice mail when Rhea's panting voice picked up. She was exercising near lunch time? Not good. If she was running midday, she was stressed. But I didn't have time to be a good friend since I was currently desperate.

"I'm about to get reamed," I whispered, making sure I was the only one in the bathroom. "I leaned on the friend, and I think someone tattled. Do you have any ammo to get me out of a hate locker?"

"What do you need?"

"Anything. Who do police think did it? Why was she killed? What was Julia into? Anything like that."

"Okay," she said, and I realized she was still running.

"Really, Rhea? Running at eleven? Do we need to have lunch and talk through some stuff?"

"First things first. Julia was killed over money, not sex. I'm sure of that. The main suspect on police radar should be the recipient of a life insurance policy Julia created ninety-three days ago."

"Her husband?" I had totally thought he was innocent.

"No. That would be the intuitive recipient of a life insurance policy. But she made the policy out to a man who isn't related to her in any way by the name of Gabriel Wilson. He's a known drug dealer, so that alone set off flags when the lead detective subpoenaed the policy."

A non-relative? That made no sense. "Why would she make someone like that the recipient?"

"I'll send you an article that explains my theory. What else do you need?"

"More on the money. Why did Julia need it? Because I'm assuming she wasn't planning on actually dying like that."

"That's pretty hazy ground," Rhea confessed. "Julia and Abel seemed to deal mostly in cash and money orders. They had a bank account, but it doesn't tell much of a story. Whatever their money habits, they were off grid, which means their debt is too. How did it go with the friend?"

"She tried to get her dog to bite me."

"She's scared," Rhea said as if I should have expected as much. "Did you convince her?"

"Maybe. I need a computer. She talked about a cave and a journal seven miles up Little Cottonwood Canyon. I'm going got check it out."

"That was smart of Julia. You taking someone with you?"

"Yeah, I was trying to get Dahl to go up with me in good will so we could get some quid pro quo going."

I knew her well enough to hear the smile in her voice. "Interesting choice."

"Shut up. You know it's not like that."

"But the point is that it could be. When you're around Dahl, you lean in, not away. That's big."

"That's nothing," I corrected. "We'd last seventy-two hours as a couple. Tops. Look, I have to get to Carla's office. I'll call you later."

"Sounds good."

We both hung up, and I used washing my hands as an

excuse to think for a second. I should have enough ammo to derail Carla's hate for my poaching activities. It was hard to reprimand results and ratings. Using a paper towel to open the door, I headed to her office.

"Sit!" she snapped, pointing to the chair across from her.

"I'll stand, thanks."

She didn't like that. "What are you doing out there? I'm getting complaint after complaint!"

"My job," I said simply.

"Your job is not to harass grieving friends and family in the wake of horrible tragedy."

"One friend," I said, holding up a finger. "Today I questioned one friend who knows a lot of stuff she's not telling, thereby allowing a killer to walk the streets."

She hesitated before yelling again. "Police haven't declared it a murder yet."

"They will. If it's suicide, then the life insurance policy won't pay out, and the killer can't have that, since he's the recipient. A guy by the name of Gabriel Wilson. Look him up. He has a sheet."

It was working. She didn't expect me to have answers. In fact, she was probably hoping I didn't so she could fire me. But I did, and that changed the game even if Carla didn't want to admit it.

"I'm going to get you a breaking story, Carla. And all the other stations will be scrambling. If one more thing pans out, we're in the clear. Police will have to name the suspect they're already looking at because the evidence will be overwhelming. So, you can assign me more filler stories, or you can get the exclusive on naming and apprehending Julia's murderer. Your call."

She stared at me for a moment like a cat staring down an encroaching dog. "What did we do when we hired you?" she finally huffed in frustration.

"You hired a reporter who doesn't mind getting dirty to get the job done."

She shook her head. "We're going to have to talk about this at your review."

"But not today," I said, earning another annoyed look.

"Not today. Get out of here. If you can get the story today, I'll run it. But if you come back with a bunch of nothing, I'm giving you a month of puff pieces. You'll do them all, and you won't complain."

Ouch. "Fine. Be ready to broadcast me live at ten."

"If you say so," she said as I walked out, head high. To my surprise, Nick was waiting for me. More surprising, he looked pensive. Seeing me exit, he stepped away from the wall he was leaning against.

"So?" he asked.

I paused and looked over his dejected stance. "Why the long face?"

He straightened. "Is it true? Are you fired?"

A little guffaw escaped me. "Who said that?"

"Angela. Everyone. Is it true?"

"Of course not," I said, heading back to my desk. Nick stayed right on my heels as we turned the corner to Angela's desk. She was sitting at it, which meant she wasn't at the Hernandez home and wouldn't be reporting live. Instead, she was spreading rumors.

"Nice shoes," I said, keeping my face impassive. For a moment she looked confused and then pleased I'd noticed her Cole Haan pumps. She was just morphing back into catty mode again when I finished my sentence. "I saw that sale too."

The timing was perfect. Her face flared red, and I caught the murder in her eyes just as we breezed past.

"You're a real class act, Kathryn," she yelled after me.

Nick let out a nervous breath. "You really like drama, don't you?"

Liking drama and attracting drama were two very different things. "Would you believe me if I told you that once upon a time I lived a very quiet life?"

"Not a chance," he said as we reached my desk. "So what do we do now?"

"We blow this story wide open before ten o'clock. That's what we do." I needed to check my email to see if Rhea had sent me the article she'd been talking about. I wanted to see if her theory worked with information I had.

"How?" he asked.

"I need to find a cave, and I'll probably need you to run around and grab B-roll for the story."

"What kind?"

I didn't know yet. I hadn't gotten that far. "Why don't you get me a coffee while I figure that part out?"

He raised an eyebrow at me. "How much do you think they pay me?"

"Who's helping you put a reel together so you can ask for a raise?" I asked. That shut him up and he left.

My inbox had populated with 281 new emails since I'd left that morning. Once of them had to be from Rhea. And twelve emails down on the list, there it was. Beautiful. It contained only a link to an online article, so I clicked.

FAKE FUNERAL FOR REAL PAY OUT

A former Phoenix postal worker has been convicted of defrauding insurers by collaborating to fake the death of one of the residents on his daily route. Prosecutors say that 42-year-old Randall Steinman assisted Juan Montero into faking his own death in exchange for half of the $500,000 insurance policy in which Montero made Steinman the named recipient.

The US Attorney's office says that when insurers investigated the unusual claim, several red flags indicated it to be fraudulent. Montero's alleged death took place when his home burned down, charring the body inside. With

no dental charts on record, investigators could not con-
clusively declare the body to be Montero's. Additionally,
Montero has grown children living in other parts of the
country, making his choice to name his mailman as the sole
beneficiary unlikely.

Conclusive proof of the scam was only obtained after
insurers honored the policy. Several days later Steinman
wired half the money to Mexico. When questioned,
Steinman claimed he was sending it to Montero's family
in an act of goodwill. Investigators were able to trace the
money to Montero when he used a portion of it to purchase
a beachside residence in Mexico.

Steinman's sentencing will take place on Nov. 9.
Negotiations are still underway for Montero's extradition.

I read it twice and called Rhea. This time she wasn't running. A good sign.

"Are you serious?" I asked. "Is this like a new fraud trend
or something?"

"Trend might be a strong term, but it fits this case."

"What about her kids, though?" That part didn't fit at all
with me. "Julia wouldn't want to leave them behind for any
amount of money, I would think."

"Maybe it wasn't about money for Julia," Rhea countered.
"Think about it, Kay. She left all the money in an insurance
policy to a convicted drug dealer. It takes some brain damage
on both sides to believe that's going to pay out without heavy
scrutiny, so emotions must have been high. What if she owed
him? What if she was working for him? Or her husband was?
What if some product was lost and she had to repay or the guy
was going to after her kids? With a victim like this, the options
are wide open."

"Too wide," I muttered.

"Point being, I think Julia was planning on faking her own
death and disappearing for a while until the policy paid out.
Once Wilson got his cut, Julia and her family should have been

free of whatever he had over them, and everyone could walk away. Maybe Julia got cold feet, or maybe Wilson got greedy. I have no idea, but it's a worthy theory with precedence."

"Yeah," I agreed. "I've got nothing better. Do you want to check out the cave with me?" I thought she'd jump at the opportunity, so it surprised me when she hesitated.

"What about Dahl?"

"I don't need him anymore. I have all the puzzle pieces."

"No, you need him. The second you find that journal, Wilson needs handcuffs on, or things will get very ugly very fast. Dahl's the right choice for this. Call him again."

"Fine," I agreed. "I'll give him another chance."

TEN

BEN HAD JASMINE on one leg and a girl named Jan on the other, and suffice it to say that all of their lips were occupied. I was stunned. If Mama had been in the room, she would've called down hellfire to burn the frat house of sin to the ground.

Gawking like the voyeur I was, I nearly jumped out of my skin when a finger tapped me on the shoulder. Spinning around in a fit of guilt, I came face to face with Rhea, which was doubly awkward. One, because of what was so obviously happening behind me. Two, because we hadn't really talked since I saw her chewing out my new sorority sisters. There had to be an explanation, but I wasn't sure if I wanted it yet. She was the closest thing I had to a friend in California, and I didn't want to know it if she'd been trying to sabotage me.

"This party blows," she was saying. "I think I'm taking off."

Mentally I tried to drop a curtain between myself and what was going on behind me so she wouldn't see, but when I saw her eyes move Ben's direction, I knew it was too late. The cheater had been caught, and—

"Ben's right over there. He should be able to walk you home or do anything you need."

She hadn't even blinked. Her boyfriend was less than twenty feet away, making out with two girls at the same time, and she *didn't care? I looked back to see if we were both seeing the same thing, and sure enough, the scene hadn't changed.*

I was speechless.

"Don't be afraid to ask him for anything," she said sounding tired. "He'll pull through for you."

I had no response and stepped in closer so I could whisper, "Did you two break up?"

Her mouth curved. "Break up? We broke up in high school. Ancient history."

"But," I began, but what could I say? "Why does he stare down guys that look at you too long?" Or, "Why do you two spend every waking moment together?" Or, "Then why does he always have his hands on you?"

My daddy always said that I had a good intuition, and right then it was telling me to keep my questions to myself and not rock the boat.

"Sure," I managed instead. "Sorry. And don't worry about me. There's a hundred people here. I'll be fine."

"You sure?" she asked, looking like she meant it. After the way I had been treating her for the past week, it was hard for me to believe she actually cared.

"Absolutely. Go if you want. I've got Carmina, Jasmine, and all the girls. I don't need to be babysat."

"Okay. Don't take any drinks from anyone. Promise?"

"Promise," I agreed.

"Then I'll see you in class."

I held up my drink. "See you then."

She turned then, not smiling, and not looking at anything between me and the door. Five seconds later she was gone. I looked at Ben, who was scowling at the door while Jasmine and the other girl continued to vie for his attention.

When his narrowed eyes landed on me, I wanted to disappear. The anger behind them was tangible, although I couldn't see why he should be the one fuming. Looking away, he whispered to each of the girls in turn, who both stood and went into the kitchen with him.

And I thought my life was complicated! Well, apparently Rhea's life wasn't as perfect as it first appeared to me. Or maybe it was still perfect; she just didn't have the perfect boyfriend like I'd thought. I was still trying to figure out what had just happened when Carmina came up behind me with Teri and Chantelle in tow.

"There you are. We've been looking for you!" Carmina said.

"For me?" I asked.

"Of course. We've wanted to show off our new Southern Belle. All the guys are asking about you."

My heart gave a little leap. "They are?"

"Of course. They call you 'legs.'"

"They want to know if you have a boyfriend back home," Chantelle jumped in.

"Well, yeah, sort of," I hedged. Jake wasn't a boyfriend per se. He was just the guy I was supposed to marry.

"Ditch him," Carmina said with authority. "Dan just broke up with Andrea Fitzsimmons. You should scoop him up."

Teri laughed. "Look at her, she just went pale. C'mon, Katie, he's just a boy. No reason to be nervous."

Maybe not in her eyes. I didn't know Dan very well, but I'd heard about him and knew what he expected from a girlfriend. I could feel my heart pounding in my throat.

"I think she needs a drink," Chantelle teased and handed me hers.

"No, thanks," I said waving it off. "I'm fine."

"Ah, c'mon, Katie."

All of a sudden the drink was in my hand with three pairs of eyes looking at me expectantly. I took as sip just to appease them and was surprised when I didn't taste any alcohol.

"This tastes like plain Diet Coke," I said, slightly confused.

"Of course it is," Chantelle laughed. "You're starting a fat

flush, remember? No alcohol for at least another month. What's
important is that it appears you are drinking."
 Relieved, I drained half the glass.

* * *

If I had been thinking, I would have forced Nick to
accompany Dahl and I on our little adventure. The boy had
a gift for taking tension out of a room, just as much as Dahl
carted it in by the truckload. Or at least he did when I was
around. There was the whole other easy-breezy side to him
that he brought out for people like Mindy Gibbons—a.k.a.
other Mormons.

But his prickly side may have been a blessing in disguise,
I decided as I took note of Dahl's rigid silhouette in my passenger seat. Like Rhea said, with Dahl I could lean in because
I knew he would lean away to compensate. His rigid religion
didn't allow him to grope a "woman of Babylon," and there was
something very freeing about knowing Dahl wasn't going to
end this night by propositioning me.

So why was he so tense around me?

I glanced down at his ostrich cowboy boots, knowing he
was going to regret wearing them. Hiking with no traction?
He'd be miserable. I told him as much, but he blew me off
so he deserved whatever he got. Even I had opted for actual
hiking shoes. Rhea had forced me to buy them when I moved
from L.A. and had forced me to go on several hikes since. A
change of clothes, Jason Wu this time, was hanging in the
back seat, ready for a quick change. George the image guru
would be pleased when we met at the beginning of next week,
I was sure. How could he object to me dressing like the First
Lady?

"No bars," Dahl said, holding up his phone. "You said
you'd explain when I couldn't call out."

"Yeah," I said, checking my rearview mirror. I felt like

Rhea. "So you have surveillance on Wilson, right?"

He nodded. "And you were going to explain to me how you knew about him."

"Please don't play dumb. You know exactly how I know."

"Then we need to investigate Rhea's resources," he grumbled.

"Sure. Because it's not like she's licensed or trained and hasn't sworn to use those resources within the parameters of the law or anything."

His sideways glance let me know he wasn't a fan on my sarcasm. Well, wasn't life just hard. "Look, Dahl. You're a beat cop, and she's an elite spy. If you wanted to be as good as her, you should have chosen a different career path." I had to give myself a mental high five for that one. It felt good to throw the insult back in his face.

"Whatever. Where are we going?"

"We're looking for a cave. And no, I don't know exactly where it is. I only know where to park so we can start looking."

He glanced in the passenger mirror looking west. "We're running out of sunlight for something like that. We've got three hours tops."

"We'll find it," I said easily. We had to, or I was on a month of puff pieces.

"Okay, Miss Optimistic. You got flashlights?"

I pulled a backpack from the back seat and handed it to him. "Check." The backpack included other essentials like a camera and a few bottles of water.

"What? No makeup bag?" His tone was so playful that I had to look to make sure some other man hadn't magically taken his place.

"I figured there's no one to impress." Besides, my makeup was in the back seat with my dress.

"So we're just going to wander around a mountain for three hours and look for a cave?"

"Yes," I said, pulling over. "This is where we're supposed to start."

"North or south side?"

"Um," I looked both directions, making a snap decision. "South."

"You're making that up."

"Maybe," I agreed, pointing to the slick drop-offs across the street. "But do you really think she was planning on scaling cliffs above a highway?"

He eyed the sheer face to our left. "Agreed. But either way, this is your party. I'm just here to make sure search and rescue doesn't have to life-flight you out of here."

"My hero," I said, reaching out for him to give me the backpack. He ignored the gesture and put it on himself.

"Lead on, Pocahontas."

I almost made comment about everything being just beyond the river bend, but decided it was just too cheesy. Besides, this wasn't a date. I didn't need to play nice. I needed to find a cave before nightfall, and I was no expert. I knew to look for water sources, though. Flowing water or evidence of stream beds would be a good thing to look out for, as would deposits of iron. People made careers out of finding caves. I should have called one of them instead of Dahl, but I needed him to make sure everything was on the up and up. Ideally, Google could have just handled this for me, but no one was blogging about Julia's special cave, and no enthusiasts had it on their maps.

Well, they would after today.

Surveying the side of the mountain, I veered a bit to the left before entering the tree line.

"So how are you liking Utah?" Dahl asked behind me. Was he actually making conversation?

"It's pretty," I said as a squirrel ran up a nearby tree. "Lots of nature."

"Yeah." Awkward pause. "Made any friends?"

I laughed outright. "Yeah, there was a line of applicants waiting for me when I got off the plane." What kind of stupid question was that? Mormons were famous for a lot of things: Jell-o recipes, ice cream consumption, multiple wives, non-alcoholic beverages, and missionary efforts. But they weren't known for friendliness unless they were looking to convert you. Then they could be downright neighborly.

Like Dahl was being right now . . . I sent him a suspicious look.

Was that what Dahl was doing? Guiding me into a talk about Mormon doctrine so he could turn our quest for a cave into a "missionary moment?" That's what the Mormons called them, and Dahl had served a mission before entering the military, so he'd be trained on how to create them.

Too bad I'd been trained on how to counter attack. Between my own religious upbringing and my research after the Mormons rolled Rhea into their web, I could handle any missionary they threw at me.

"Do you like living in the city?" he asked, moving well in his slick boots.

Again, I laughed. "This is not a city, Dahl. It's a glorified suburb made relevant by the hub of a major airline."

He frowned. "You must like something about Utah since you moved here."

I ducked under a branch and followed a slope to low ground. I didn't hear any water but hoped for a stream bed. "I moved here for one reason only, and it wasn't to get snuggly with the natives."

"Why then?"

Stream bed. Score! Now I just needed to follow it up to see where it connected into the mountain. "If I have to tell you that, then you're a horrible detective, Dahl." I started leading us up the hill again, following the overgrown stream bed.

"For Rhea?" he asked. "It's got to be more than that. I have friends who move to other states. I don't follow them."

He had a point, but he also didn't know what he was talking about. "Well, don't bend your brain trying to figure it out then."

Behind me I could hear his boots sliding around a bit. He was going to be totally miserable. It would be fun to see how long it took him to confess that he'd been an idiot not to wear appropriate shoes. But at least the loose terrain had shut him up for the moment. Like most men, he couldn't concentrate on more than one thing at once.

"Are you going home for the holidays?"

Okay, that cinched it. Dahl was definitely in missionary mode. "No. You?"

"Maybe Christmas. Why aren't you going home?"

"Because I'm a bottom-of-the-totem-pole reporter," I said, using a branch to pull me up a steep incline. "Anything else you want to know?"

He missed a step but caught himself before falling. "Hey, I'm just trying to make nice here."

I stopped to face him. "No, you're BRT-ing."

His face read of clear shock. "W-what?"

"Building a relationship of trust," I defined for him, even though I didn't have to. He knew the term. Mormons had made it up themselves. "You're establishing common ground between us before easing into a subject like the Book of Mormon."

"Or I'm just trying to get to know you," he shot back. For a moment I second guessed myself. But no, his larynx had hiked when he denied it, and I had been friends with a private investigator too long to miss something as obvious as voice pitching.

"Dahl, I've lived here over a month and you've never once taken an effort to be social—even when we went on our Teton adventure. So don't think I'll buy that line now." I turned and started back up the mountain. "And it's fine. We can talk about your church if you want to. I probably know more about it than you do."

He laughed, clearly convinced otherwise. "Uh, yeah. Not possible."

"Watch it. My granddaddy is an Evangelical preacher. Every third Sunday we had classes on Combating Mormonism during Sunday school. Believe me when I say I have a black belt in the art."

"Granddaddy?" he echoed, honing in on that over everything else. Westerners didn't use terms like that, but that was their deal. I couldn't say grandpa any more than they'd say granddaddy.

"Yes, you got a problem with that?"

I could hear the smile in his voice. "No. It's just endearing is all. Sometimes when you say certain words, you have a weird little lilt in your voice. Like an accent."

Not good. Had I been getting lazy? Normally Rhea would tell me if I was, but we hadn't been spending that much time together since I was on constant overtime.

"Where are you from?" he asked.

For a second I panicked, wondering how much of the truth to share. Then I remembered that Dahl was a cop. It would take him ten seconds on a company computer to find the answer to that question. And if he hadn't already done it himself, coworkers certainly had. He was asking questions he already knew the answers to.

"You seriously expect me to believe that you don't already know? Why don't you just admit that you've already done a background check on me, and we'll just start from there."

I couldn't see his face since I was in front, but I could tell he was readjusting his sails. "Have you looked me up?" He sounded nervous.

"Of course I have." I turned and gave him a playful wink.

"I've got to know what I'm getting myself into when I invite a man up into the mountains."

He didn't smile back. "So you know about my divorce?"

"The one blemish on your record? Yeah. Although, let's face it, that one was a little bit out of your hands." After no reply from him, I glanced back and saw something akin to shame on his face.

"I should have written her more."

I stopped to face him, only to have him run into me from behind. We both moved apart as I eyed him, trying to see if he really believed something so idiotic.

"Do you honestly think that if you had written a few more letters, your wife wouldn't have shacked up with another man?"

"She said she felt abandoned."

"Uh-huh. And how about you sleeping out in a desert under constant threat of gunfire while she stayed in a nice condo? If you ask me, she was just needy and bored. You two were what, twenty-three when you got married?"

"I was twenty-three. She was twenty," he corrected.

I threw my hands up in the air as if that explained it all. "So you come home from one of those Mormon missions and enlist in the military for some reason only you can understand—"

"I prayed about it," he snapped.

"Of course you did," I said, knowing I sounded condescending as I made my way to my point. "Once enlisted, you find a goody-goody girl who's never missed a week of church and secretly lets you get to second base. She loves your body and loves the idea of having a husband all her friends covet—"

"That's not—"

"I'm not finished. You two sprint to a temple marriage, and it's only once you're living with her that you sense you may have jumped the gun. But by then you're deployed, which makes both of you become a fantasy to each other again. You barely make it through the first deployment. By the time you're redeployed, she feels single again. And by the time you're gone a third time, she's replaced you and got pregnant with the other guy to seal the deal." I sent him a look to let him know I was done. "Sound about right?"

He looked down at his boots. "Maybe something like that."

"Twenty," I said, pressing on. "That was your problem. And it wasn't like you really knew her, right?"

"I knew her!" His emphatic objection had Rhea's words playing in my head. People who answered a question with more emotion than it was asked with were usually harboring guilt.

"Fine," I said, holding a branch back for him. "Prove it. What size jeans did she wear?"

"Jeans?" he echoed. "I don't know. I didn't pay attention to that stuff."

"Which means you never bought her clothes," I pointed out.

"I got her other things."

"Like?"

"She liked to eat out," he said. "She liked flowers and jewelry."

"Smart girl," I said, hoping he'd had the taste to get her something good in that last category. "So say it's your anniversary. Where would you take her to eat?"

"I don't know. Wherever she wanted."

A disgusted noise escaped me. "Really, Dahl? A pointer for your next anniversary with your next wife: women don't want you to make them choose their favorite restaurant. They want you to know their favorite restaurant and surprise them with reservations."

"Some women like to choose," he retorted, and I shook my head, knowing he could see it from behind.

"Not any woman you would date."

He stopped this time. "That's not a fair assessment. You don't know me."

I kept walking, wondering just how far the stream bed went. All the way up the mountain? Was I in the wrong area entirely? Probably. "I know you better than you know me. And I definitely know enough to see how much estrogen you're able to handle."

"I doubt that."

No point in arguing over that. "Okay." We hiked for about thirty seconds in silence before he spoke again.

"It was her high school boyfriend."

"Your wife's baby daddy?"

"Ex-wife," he clarified.

"Sorry. Ex-wife."

"She connected with him on Facebook, and they started going to the same parties while I was in Afghanistan. They had a big history together. She told me she'd always been in love with him. They'd dated all through high school but had broken up at graduation because their values were too different."

I tried not to chuckle. "Meaning he wasn't Mormon, right?"

Dahl hesitated. "No. He wasn't. So she tried to forget him by marrying me. At least that's what she said when she gave me the divorce papers."

Ouch. Seriously, that had to hurt. "That sucks, Dahl."

"Yeah," he agreed. "Anyway, they're married now."

"Mazel tov."

To my relief, he actually laughed. "You know, as brusque as you are, you're pretty easy to talk to."

"Uh-huh. Remember that the next time you accuse me of plotting mercenary interviews with grieving husbands." I paused, spotting a tiny inlet to our stream bed, and Dahl nearly knocked me over.

"Whoa," he said, pulling me to him so I wouldn't fall.

"Sorry," I stammered. "I need to say something when I

stop like that, but I'm starting to think the bed we're in goes for miles even though the cave should be in this area somewhere."

"Agreed." Only when he spoke did I realize that his hands were still on me. And the moment I noticed, he seemed to realize it as well and quickly dropped them to his sides. For a moment I was stunned. He had touched me—no, grabbed me—and I hadn't even noticed. My chest hadn't clamped in panic . . . my stomach hadn't cramped with anxiety.

All systems were normal.

"I, uh . . ." What were we talking about? "I was thinking about heading up to find the source of this little guy."

He gestured into the thick brush. "Like I said, this is your little party."

I looked at his boots. "Your feet doing okay?"

"Oh, I'm feeling every rock, but I'll make it."

"Nice. As long as you admit that I was right."

"Yes, Kathryn," he said like a dutiful student. "You were right."

"Excellent," I said, starting up. "And sorry about all the thick underbrush. I know it will make it harder for you to watch my butt while we hike."

"I'll try to survive. I promise I will only glance up frequently enough to remind myself why I talk to you at all."

His sarcastic humor was so out of the blue that it got a full belly laugh out of me. "You keep talking like that, Dahl, and we just might get along."

"Well, then. I'll try to abstain."

"Do that," I agreed. "It will be easier for all." But the damage had been done. Dahl could be funny? With me? And he hadn't brought up his church yet? I wouldn't have thought it possible.

"You know, you don't suck at this," he said as if surprised.

"At what?"

"Looking for a cave," he clarified. "Granted, I have no

idea if you're doing a single thing right, but the fact that you can even walk on this terrain without tripping is more than I expected."

Wow. The man didn't even know when he was being painfully condescending. "So let me get this straight. You're impressed that I can walk up a mountain and not fall down?"

"Well, when you say it like—"

"I'm just saying what you said. But at least now I'm starting to understand why you think I'm such a bad reporter. What else can I do to impress you? Turn on a stove?"

"Ha-ha," he deadpanned. "You know what I mean. Most women like you won't even step off a sidewalk. I've definitely never seen one trail blaze."

"That's because you only date women who follow you." Oh, snap! This conversation was actually starting to get fun.

"No offense, Kathryn, but you have no idea the kind of women I like to date."

I couldn't leave that alone. "That's because there's a huge stretch between who you would like to date and who you actually date. It's the difference between 'should' and 'want.' It's why you let me kiss you up in the Tetons. I was your short little walk on the wild side of 'want.' "

"Not true!" Once again, his denial was more heated than my accusation. Guilty.

I shot him a raised eyebrow. "No? What was I then?"

"I . . . ah . . ." I had him there. It felt good. I didn't even care what his answer was. All that mattered was that he was afraid of it. "You surprised me."

"Oh, I surprised you so you made out with me for ten minutes?"

"Five," he corrected.

I clicked my tongue at him. "Time flies when you're having fun. It was ten."

His abrupt discomfort was tangible in the air, putting

wind in my sails. "We shouldn't talk about that."

"Why? Because you'll want to do it again, or because you think it's something you should be ashamed of?" Or both. I didn't mention option number three, which was why I was surprised to hear him say it.

"Both." The boy got bonus points for honesty. "I don't kiss women I don't know. Kissing should mean something."

It had meant something. At least to me. Maybe not when I first threw myself at him it hadn't. I'd done that partly out of curiosity and mostly just to knock his socks off before getting back to business as usual by brushing him off. I called it my "catch and release" move. Giving men a taste and then walking away made them more malleable in future interactions.

But after five seconds, I had realized the same thing I'd noticed just a few minutes ago when Dahl had grabbed me: it didn't hurt. It was like some miraculous time warp had happened, allowing me to go back in time to when kissing a guy was still a fantasy, not an irrational fear. And in those short minutes where our lips stayed connected, I proved something I had only suspected based on how I felt with Ben and Isaac— that it wasn't a man's touch that made me ill, it was how he touched me. His intent.

A girl can experiment a lot in ten minutes. I'd pushed in, pulled away, teased, and played. I'd been the aggressor and a core part of me had understood that no matter what I did, Dahl would not go to bed with me any more than Ty would. His eyes weren't going to get that steely focus while his breath grew shallow and he pushed me against the nearest hard object.

It wouldn't happen. And knowing that liberated something in me.

"What? No snappy retort this time?" he asked.

"Nope," I said, pushing through two bushes that had grown into each other. We were approaching the mountain face. I crossed my fingers and hoped against hope that I had been inspired and that we'd walk into the mouth of a cave.

Dahl wasn't ready to drop it. "It's just . . . to be honest, I'd never kissed anyone who wasn't Mormon before."

The guy should just stop talking. I could only handle so many unintentional insults before lighting his hair on fire. "And was it as damning as you imagined it would be?"

"Now you're just being ridiculous."

Was I? Because I certainly wasn't being Pocahontas. When I walked us up to a wall of shale, there was no cave. Even worse, the sun was behind our horizon line. We were going to lose light a lot faster than I planned on. I didn't want to admit this to Dahl, though, so I stuck to the subject at hand.

"Well, in all fairness, it was the first time I kissed a Mormon, and I didn't burst into flame either. I guess we're even." Red soil. Water outlets. I searched up, down and all around looking for a hint on what direction would be best to go. If Rhea were here, she would know. Then again, Rhea would have found some topical map or something and deduced where the cave was before heading up the mountain. Then she would have walked straight to it and grabbed her prize without breaking a sweat.

Why hadn't I brought her?

On any other day and any other planet I would have, but the truth was, I'd been curious. Yes, I'd come up with other reasons, but really I just wanted to know if what I'd felt for ten minutes in Jackson Hole was a fluke before Dahl disappeared into a world where our paths would never cross. I wanted to kiss him again.

Poor guy. He'd probably already repented for the last time. Maybe it wasn't worth forcing. Maybe I should just leave well enough alone. Maybe I should concentrate on finding a cave while Dahl furrowed his brow and tried to figure out a response to me joking about bursting into flames.

Then it hit me. I was looking at this all wrong. I'd been looking for a cave—something I had no idea how to do—

when I really should be tracking Julia. She'd been here recently, which meant she left some sort of trail. That's what I should have looked for from the beginning.

Well, it was too late to start over now.

"I don't think it damns me to kiss someone who isn't LDS. I just don't see the point of it since I'm not going to marry someone outside of my faith. What's the point in getting all those feelings started?"

I scanned the terrain, looking for shoes marks. "So you're saying that you only kiss women when you see wife potential in them?"

"There's nothing wrong with that."

"I'm not judging." My heart wasn't in the conversation anymore, and I think he noticed because he got all pouty and folded his arms. This was the Dahl I knew.

"It's getting dark."

"We've got time," I said. No tracks moved along the base of the incline, which had me reassessing the shale. Sure, rocks had shifted around up there recently, but anything could have done that. Wind, animals, gravity.

"In this neck of the woods?" he grumbled. "We've got thirty minutes of light, tops."

I sent him a dirty look. "What's the male version of Debby Downer, because you're him." I gestured down the mountain. "Go wait in the car if you want—if you can find it."

"So you can get lost?"

I rolled my eyes. "If you're going to insult me, at least try to be accurate. We both know I won't get lost. Now come on. We're going up." It was a snap decision, mostly made for an excuse not to have to stand next to him when he brought marriage up again.

"Up that rock slide?" he asked.

"You're welcome to wait down here," I said, taking the first few steps.

"No," he said. "Because I really do want to talk to you

about the Church, if you say you know so much about it."

"Even though you don't think I do," I clarified, choosing my steps carefully so as not start a rock slide.

His boot slipped, but he caught himself with his hand. "That remains to be seen."

I had to know. "Is that why you came up here? You figured if all else failed, we could talk about this?"

He shrugged. "It's just weird. You move to Utah, your best friend is Mormon, so is her fiancé and everyone I see you with, and yet you're not. Why not?"

"Because I don't believe any church has the exclusive right on truth. Next question?"

"Truth is everywhere," he said, cherry picking his steps. "Every religion has elements of truth."

"Not really," I said as we neared the top. "There's some messed up stuff out there."

"Truth can be perverted into something it was never meant to be."

I pursed my lips, wondering if he really understood what he'd just said. "You said it, not me."

"Do you believe in God?" he asked as my feet hit solid ground again. No more shifting shale.

"I tried not to for a while, but I have a friend who makes that impossible." I glanced around, almost picking a direction at random before I saw tracks—actual tracks. One person. They could belong to anyone at all, but a pair of sneakers had dug in looking for traction as they'd moved up the mountain. Excited, I followed the trail.

Dahl was right behind me like a shark that smelled blood. "Do you pray?"

"Never."

"Have you read the Bible?"

"From beginning to end?" I clarified. He nodded. "Nine times."

"Nine?" he echoed in disbelief.

"I'm a preacher's granddaughter." The tracks were clear and easy to follow. Even better, they were small—maybe a size six in women's shoes. There was hope I was on the right path.

"And the Book of Mormon?"

I held up three fingers, letting them speak for me.

"Three times? All the way through?"

"Yep. Plus your Doctrine and Covenants, Pearl of Great Price, Lectures on Faith, and a bunch of other Mormon books."

He didn't believe me. It was written all over his face. "Why would you do all that?"

I kept my eye on the trail and not on him. "A cult abducted my best friend. Why wouldn't I learn everything I could about it?"

"Yeah, but usually people just stick to the anti-Mormon literature."

"Oh, I read that too."

He was still stuck on my first claim about the Book of Mormon. "Three times?"

"Cover to cover," I affirmed. "Go ahead. Quiz me." We were moving closer to solid rock face, and in about ten minutes we might have to turn on the flashlights. Once we did that, Dahl would want to turn back, unless I kept him talking. "Seriously. If you don't think I read, then stump me."

The look on his face was priceless, but in the end his curiosity won over. "Fine. Who was Nephi?"

"Ha! Trick question. There was more than one." I gave myself a mental point.

"Okay. Opinion question, then. What's your favorite story?"

"Hmmm," I debated. "This is also a trick question. You're trying to trick me into saying I liked something about the Book of Mormon." He looked all put out for a second before I back pedaled and gave him a little smile. "No, seriously. That

Captain Moroni guy sounded like he knew how to get things done. I'd pick him probably, even though he's like a Republican on steroids."

"Okay. However that makes sense."

"Oh, please. He rides around rallying people to join his army and killing the ones who won't fight for their country? He definitely wasn't a Democrat."

In a nice change of pace, Dahl actually laughed. "I had never divided people in the Book of Mormon into political parties before. Who does that?"

I shrugged, a little embarrassed. "It helps me remember them."

He had a silly grin on his face. "So were any of them Democrats then?"

"Sure. The younger Alma. The sons of Mosiah. Once they got something they wanted to share it with everyone equally. All the Ammonites. Everyone after Jesus allegedly visited. Then there were libertarians like King Benjamin—"

He was laughing so hard he had to stop walking. I didn't. I kept plugging right along.

"Man," he breathed and then trotted after me. "I have to share that with my parents. That would be a heated discussion."

"Whatever. We need to climb." The change of subject couldn't have come at a better moment. We'd reached the end of the trail and it walked straight into a short twenty-foot cliff.

"Sun's almost gone," he said with a trace of laughter still in his voice.

"So we'll hurry. You should wait down here with those boots. You'll need grip coming down." I didn't wait for his reply. I just started up while he debated. Like he said, we didn't have much light to work with and a month's worth of puff pieces hung in the balance.

ELEVEN

DAN'S BEEN TALKING *about you," Carmina said. "You could probably land him tonight if you wanted to, but you need to move fast before Andrea weasels her way back in."*

"Yeah," Teri agreed. "She can't go twenty-four hours without a boyfriend. So insecure!"

I tried to act like I was interested in what they were saying, but the truth was that I was starting to feel a little nervous. I couldn't put my finger on it, but something just seemed off. I rationalized that it was all the talk about Dan, a guy I barely knew by sight, and the pressure to seduce him. And although that idea did fill with a hint of dread, there was something else I couldn't quite my finger on.

"He's downstairs. Do you want to go see him?" Chantelle asked, enthusiastically pulling my arm to follow her.

"Really, you guys, I'm fine. I've got a great guy back home."

"And he's not seeing other girls while you're away?" Carmina snorted. "Get real if you believe that."

"Just come look," Teri pressed. "It's like window shopping. Looking never hurt anyone."

My heart said no, but the part of me that wanted to fit in won over.

"Fine, just a look," I agreed. "Nothing more."

All three of them nodded their heads excitedly and dragged me down into the basement. Then Carmina pulled back a floor rug to reveal a trap door and stomped her foot on it three times. It was only a split second before the floor opened up and a frat boy popped his head out.

"Dost thou bring an offering to the gods?" he intoned, then his eyes landed on me. "Ah, we've been waiting. Welcome."

Okay. That was weird, but none of the other girls seemed to think so, so I didn't say anything.

He held out his hand to me first. "A help down for the lady?"

Smiling back, I took his hand and let it steady me as I took my first steps down the hidden set of stairs.

"Kay, right?" he asked as I brushed past him.

"Yeah," I replied a little breathlessly, so pleased that he knew my name that I forgot to ask him his. I nearly forgot him entirely when I got a look at his "secret lair." It looked like a fight club illuminated entirely by fire. There had to be nearly thirty frat boys lounging around, and we must have been the first girls invited because I didn't see any other females around.

My eyes were drawn to the center of the room, where a large square was carved into the stone like hallowed ground. Carved symbols gave the little arena an odd sort of pagan look, which was only enhanced by the heavy percussion music that filled the room. I made a mental note to stay away from the arena, since I'd heard that fraternities could be superstitious about such things. The last thing I wanted to do was be known as the girl who disrupted their shrine, or whatever it was.

"Drink?" a rather good-looking guy said, holding out a cup to me.

"I've got my own," I said, holding out my trusty Diet Coke.

He smiled a very sexy smile. "Let me know if you need to be topped off."

"Will do," I agreed, and took a sip of my drink just to be social as I waited for Carmina, Teri, and Chantelle to join me. They seemed to be taking their time up at the top.

"Do you want to dance?" the good-looking guy asked. A glance around revealed some of the guys leering at me. This guy felt way safer, so I nodded.

"Sure, just let me figure out a place to put this," I said, holding out my drink.

"Just chug it," he said, his eyes seductive. "It's almost gone anyway."

I did, and watched as he gently took the plastic cup away from me and dropped it with flourish. Smooth, I thought as he led me away from the stairs and to the main floor. I felt like every eye was on me when he gently pulled me into his arms, surprisingly keeping a gentleman's distance.

"So you're Kay Griswold," he murmured against my ear. "I've heard a lot about you."

"You have?" I asked in surprise.

"Of course," he said easily. "The first time I heard that sexy drawl of yours, I knew I had to know more about you, so I made it my business to find out."

It was a line, but it worked. I blushed. "And what did you find out?"

"Hmm?" he said, lazily looking at my lips. "Forgive me if I can't really remember now that I have you in my arms."

I didn't know how to respond to that. I was flattered. At the same time, I felt like melting into him . . . holding on to him . . . leaning into him . . . touching him. I looked down at my hands, which seemed to hang more than hold on to my dance partner. That was odd.

I might have stood there swaying with him for two or twenty minutes, I'm not quite sure. All I knew was that I was confused by these new sensations that were so different than anything I had experienced in the past. Bells of alarm rang in my head as I realized that something was wrong. I wasn't thinking like my usual self, and I felt my mind shutting off, even as something else took over. I tried to draw away but found my face snuggled into his neck.

"You smell good," I heard myself say, and then my mind swirled. I felt cold stone against my back. Heard a distant sound that sounded like cheering. Above me shadows played on the ceiling as I felt my hands pulled over my head. I tried to pull them back down to where they belonged, but forgot what I was doing when they didn't move and something bound them tightly together.

"Ow," I muttered, trying to pull them apart again. I might as well have tried to lift a car. I couldn't even open my eyelids to see what was pulling me off the ground into a standing position. Then my feet weren't touching the ground anymore. Nothing was.

I was hanging?

Forcing my eyes open, I saw blur of shapes around me. One figure held a torch, which he touched to the ground. The entire perimeter of the arena burst into flames, and a chorus of voices started some chant. My eyes fell shut again. The slight swing of my body would have lulled me to sleep except for the pinch on my wrists that grew more and more painful.

Then a soft cloth covered my face and everything went dark.

* * *

The climb to the cave wasn't really a difficult one going up, but I took note that it would be tricky coming down in the dark. Several of the foot holds would have to be found blind. In less than a minute I was on the top and seeing exactly what I wanted to see—what I hadn't dared hope to see. I reached for my camera only to realize it was in the bag on Dahl's back twenty feet below.

"Dahl, get up here," I called down. "I need that bag."

"Are you serious? There's a cave up there?"

"Yep," I said, looking around for animal tracks. Last thing I wanted was to walk into to some animal's home. I didn't see any evidence that anything had taken residence nearby, so I walked toward the opening.

A few seconds later Dahl pulled himself over the ledge and joined me.

"Holy cow," he breathed. "I didn't think we'd find a thing up here."

"How about that camera and the flashlights?" I said, holding out my hand. "Let's check out the inside."

Pulling the backpack off, he fished out the flashlights. I grabbed the camera, and we crept forward. Nothing caught my attention until I entered the cave and swept the beam to the right. About fifteen feet away lay my own personal jackpot. I raised the camera and started shooting.

"Backpack," I said, taking inventory as I moved in for closer shots. "Sleeping bag, a large cooler and," using my sleeve to cover my hand, I picked up a picture frame. "Bingo!" My flashlight showed the picture was of Julia and her children. It was a candid photo, a captured moment of honest happiness where everyone was in varying stages of laughter. It was heart breaking.

"Careful not to rub," Dahl instructed. "We'll want prints off of that."

I took it toward the entrance of the cave to see the picture without the glare of my flashlight, but the deep orange hues of the sunset only made the picture more haunting. The woman I was looking at was dead. Why? Was Rhea right? Had she made a deal with a local drug dealer to get out of some kind of trouble and ended up paying with her life?

It wasn't long before Dahl came up behind me, his voice coaxing me out of my reverie. "You okay?"

"I need to get Nick up here," I said, not answering his question while pulling out my phone. It proudly displayed that I had no signal. "Does your phone work?"

He checked and shook his head. "Nope. No bars."

"Damn," I muttered, watching him flinch at the curse. As much as I talked a tough game against his values, there was something adorable about a man who shuddered at unsavory words.

"It's getting dark fast, Kathryn. We've got to get moving."

"Yeah," I agreed. "But there's supposed to be a journal up here. We need that so you can call in the arrest for our killer. I'm not leaving without that."

"We shouldn't disturb the scene."

I held up the picture. "Already did, officer. And I'm not leaving without the smoking gun. Oh, and I need you to tell me where that's going to go down so I can get my cameraman there to film it."

"Kathryn—"

"I'm handing you a killer," I warned. "The least you can do is hand me a photo op. "

"That's not how it works, and you know it."

"I also know that I'll get Nick to the scene with or without your help, but I sure would like you more as a human being if you didn't make my life hard just this once." I let him chew on that as I moved back into pitch black cave and set the picture back where I'd found it. The intuitive place to put a journal was in the backpack so I turned my attention to that. Again, I used my sleeve to cover my prints. Rhea was religious about not leaving prints, and she made me paranoid like her.

"Kathryn, it's getting pretty dark out there."

"One sec." I filtered through the contents, including a folder holding a copy of her life insurance policy. A big point to Rhea on that one. The journal would tell if she was right on all accounts. At least I hoped it would as I pulled it out. Taking a breath, I opened it, ready to learn the truth.

It was in Spanish. Page after page of Spanish, which I didn't speak a lick of.

"Seriously?" I protested.

"What?" Dahl said moving in behind me, then chuckled. "Nice. We have guys who can translate for us."

"Maybe Wilson's name is in here," I muttered, flipping the pages.

"We'll take it with us and look at it in the car while driving to the station. We've got to use the light we have and get down."

"Fine," I said, putting the journal in my pack. "Let's book it then." I took one last picture before putting the camera away as well.

"Can you find this area again?" he asked.

"Can't you?" I replied, honestly curious.

"Probably not in the dark."

"Huh. Yeah, I could find it. Or they could bring police dogs. They'd find the trail too."

He shouldered the pack, and we turned toward our downward climb. It was pitch black. The glow of light on the horizon did nothing to illuminate it.

For a moment, we both just peered over the edge. There was no way down—especially in Dahl's boots, but it took him about two minutes longer to come to that conclusion than it did for me. His realization was punctuated by him kicking a rock over the edge and down the abyss.

"We're stuck," he grumbled. "What are we supposed to do now?"

I looked over at his strong profile and remembered the thought process that had brought him up there with me to begin with.

"We could always make out," I teased, enjoying how he tensed at the suggestion.

"I'm being serious here, Kathryn!"

I shrugged as if to say, *Me too.*

"It's dark, and we have no supplies," he grumbled, making a grocery list of our woes. "It's going to get cold. Really cold. We have no food—and no, we're not touching Maria's supply. It's evidence."

The worry lines on his face were adorable. "Ah, c'mon," I said. "I'm not made of glass. It's not like I've never slept on the ground before."

"Have you?"

I moved back toward the cave to get away from the ledge. "Of course I have. Everyone was a kid once, Dahl. Now let's gather some kindling for a fire. I'm pretty sure I saw some in there, and it's not like you need firewood for evidence. It'll keep us warm. And if we're super lucky, someone will spot it."

He didn't move. "I didn't see a lighter in there. What are we going to do with the wood once we get it? You have a pack of matches I don't know about?"

For once in my life it would have been handy to be a smoker. "No, but I do have a shoelace."

"And what do you plan to do with that?"

I smiled through a frown. "They didn't teach you how to bow drill in Scouts? I'm disappointed in the system."

He looked incredulous. "With a shoelace? Yeah, that's not happening."

"I'll look for matches in her stuff. You get kindling." I moved into the cave without waiting for his reply so he went get busy gathering twigs on our ledge. Careful to return things where I found them, I searched for a lighter, matches, anything, and saw nothing until I discovered a little ledge naturally formed into the wall. It held a small lighter. Looked like I wouldn't be bow drilling after all.

Walking out, I shined a light on my find so Dahl would see and maybe not freak as much before outlining a fire pit with nearby rocks. I couldn't see the road, which meant no one heading up the mountain would see us. Not unless they were flying over.

By the time the fire was crackling, Dahl was silent and I was nervous. I needed to hit my deadline. Happily, I had about three hours to do so, but being stuck up a mountain did nothing to help. I chewed on my bottom lip and tried to decide whether or not to ditch Dahl and try getting down the mountain myself. It would be a no-brainer if it weren't for the drop off just a few feet away.

"You cold?" Dahl asked.

I opened my mouth to say no but hesitated. We were sitting next to each other, and I didn't feel nauseated. If I was ever going to get a repeat opportunity to experiment with Dahl, this would be it.

I gave my arms a little rub. "A little."

"You want my jacket?" he asked, offering his Stetson.

We were close. I wanted him closer. "Then you'll be cold."

He bought the ploy, concern pulling at his features. The guy was 200 pounds of muscle trained to take down big, bad guys, and in that moment, it looked like his biggest concern in the world was that I might start shivering.

"I'm fine. I don't get cold easy." Yet he'd worn a jacket this whole time.

He handed me the coat and got to working feeding our little fire while I put on. It smelled like him, since he was a Stetson man through and through. Very Indiana Jones. But putting on his coat alone was a test. No matter how good a man smelled, I couldn't stand having his scent on me. Nothing could get me into a shower faster than traces of my date's cologne lingering in the air around me, but I wasn't gagging. I was okay.

"Better?" he asked.

"Much," I said and meant it.

We watched the fire, both lost in our own thoughts.

"There's a chance we'll be here all night," he said.

"A chance," I agreed, although I'd already decided to go down on my own. I'd wait it out a little bit and play around with the moment, but I was not sleeping up there and missing my deadline.

"I suppose we should talk," he ventured.

I gave a little chuckle. "Sure. We could try that again."

"So . . ." He fidgeted, adjusting his sitting position.

I picked the safest subject I could think of. "So, what's your favorite color?"

He turned to look at me, his face inches from mine. "Are you serious?"

I shrugged. "I guess not. I already know."

"You do?"

"Sure."

His eyes narrowed with skepticism. "Fine, what is it?"

"Blue."

His lips pressed together and his eyes stayed skeptical. "That's probably the favorite color of half the men on this planet."

"Maybe," I agreed. "But the point is that it's yours, and I knew it. I bet you don't know my favorite color."

"Couldn't begin to guess." Nor did he ask, so it seemed awkward to volunteer the information. His eyes met mine. "We didn't really finish that conversation earlier, did we? What else do you know about me?"

I gave him one of my trademark sly looks. "Anything I want to know."

He laughed. "I'll bet!"

"But you're the one who didn't fess up last time. What dirt did you and your coworkers dig up on me?"

"Just a basic check," he said quickly. "Nothing big."

"And what did you find out?"

He hesitated, watching the flames dance for several seconds before replying. "You grew up in Alabama and attended school at UCLA, and your real last name isn't McCoy."

"And?" I prompted. As a cop he would have seen more if he looked up my old name too. He would have seen everything.

"And you've talked your way out of every speeding ticket."

"And?" I prompted again.

He shrugged. "Your sheet's pretty boring."

No. It wasn't. I had a very significant court record he had to have seen if he looked up my old name—unless someone had scrubbed my name from it. And I just so happened to know someone who might have taken it upon herself to make that happen without whispering a word.

I would have to ask Rhea about that.

At the moment, all I cared about was that Dahl didn't know. He had no idea about my past other than the belief that I'd breezed through life with a fast pass.

"Well, some of us have to be boring, I guess," I said.

I was still comfortable. The cologne wasn't making me gag, I hadn't flung the coat into the fire, and in the moments where we brushed up against each other, I actually found it pleasant.

"I know you're going to hate me for this, but I've got to try it." Then I leaned in and kissed him, ready for him to yank away. I wasn't wife material, after all. He'd said so himself. Kissing me was disingenuous.

All that said, it felt just as good as I had remembered it. Rather than pounding in my head, my heart gave lazy pulls in my chest, warming my blood. A small amount of trepidation pooled in my stomach, but that might have been from worry about missing my deadline.

Then he pulled away. "Kathryn, this isn't—"

I stopped his lips with my finger. "I'm not trying to seduce you. I just want to see if last time was a fluke." That was all the explanation I gave before leaning back in. The fact that he didn't stop me made me wonder if maybe he'd felt something different too. Maybe I'd ask him another time. Not now. Not when I was fighting against wrapping my arms around his neck and crying with joy.

I wasn't broken. I could respond to a man's touch as long as it wasn't pushing. And given who I was, how I dressed, and the men I chose to be with, I'd always been pushed. It retrospect, it was easy to see how I'd trapped myself into a pattern of being objectified. I'd done it because I wanted control over the men. That and a reason to hate them. And given that I had to be slightly drunk to sleep with a man, it was really easy to hate him the next morning and convince myself he'd taken advantage of me when I really thrown myself to a wolf.

But no, there was hope for me. Twice was a pattern, not a fluke. After years of wondering, Dahl had finally answered that mystery for me. I wanted to pull him in and hold him close, just because I could. I wanted to test his limits to see how far they really went—and how far I went with them.

"You're a really good kisser," he said, angling in. If that was true, it was blind luck because I certainly wasn't thinking about technique. I was too busy having a revelation.

Next to us I felt the fire cooling, but we chose not to care. Let it go out. I'd start it again. More important things were at hand, such as curbing the desire to put my hand somewhere that would freak Dahl out. He would yank everything to a halt unless I kept my hands to myself.

He would stop us.

Who knew that would make all the difference to me?

When his hand hesitantly gripped my waist, I braced for the worst, and it never came. All of a sudden, the world felt warm again, as if the fire next to us had spontaneously reignited.

"Ken," I whispered, using his first name for some unknown reason. "This is amazing."

His lips curved. "Did you just say that with a Southern accent?"

Had I? Well, how about that? Instead of replying, I just kissed him again.

I couldn't tell you how long we sat there defying the laws of natural attraction by keeping things slow and steady when I felt my left side grow hot. It was an odd thing to notice, but it seemed like the fire was getting stronger with time instead of dying down. Worried we might be starting a forest fire, I snuck a look back and nearly jumped out of my skin.

Five feet away, crouching next to the fire and patiently feeding it, was Rhea. I jerked away from Dahl before he realized what was going on, and he jumped up, ready for the worst.

"Rhea!" I breathed, both relieved and blushing. "How in the world did you find us?"

She had the grace to look bashful. "Sorry. I didn't mean to interrupt. The fire was just dying and didn't want you to get cold."

"Not a problem," I muttered.

"How did you find us?" Dahl asked, looking more than a little flustered himself.

"I saw the fire," she said, as if it were obvious. "Isn't that one of the reasons you lit it?"

"I should've known," I laughed. "Tell me you have a magical way down the twenty-foot cliff face that stands between us and freedom."

She took off her backpack, unzipped it, and threw a rope across the fire to me. "You're free birds," she said before offering a sly smile. "But I understand if you want to be stranded just a little longer."

I don't know if Dahl blushed, but I did. The blush changed to disappointment, though, when he picked up the rope and went to search for a place to tie it off.

TWELVE

I **AWOKE TO THE** *spray of sprinklers and heat of the sun. The former had me gasping for breath, and the latter gave me the vague awareness that it was morning. My hands flew up to protect my face from the jetting stream, but when I started to roll away from it, a sharp pain had me gasping for breath and inhaling some water in the process. My arms felt fine, and from the knees down my legs felt fine, but everything in between felt like it had been battered by a gauntlet. I tried to move again and felt a sob escape my throat.*

What was wrong with me?

Over the methodical hissing of the sprinklers, another sound caught my attention. Not the singing birds, because that was a sound you expected to hear when you awake outside under the rain of sprinklers. Laughter.

Guarding my eyes, I looked around and immediately recognized my surroundings. I was on the front lawn of the sorority house. How in the world had I gotten there? Had I passed out? Had I . . . why couldn't I remember even leaving the party the night before?

I could still hear the laughing.

Maybe I would be laughing too if I saw a sorority sister passed out on the front lawn, but nothing seemed funny since parts of me

I didn't know existed were shouting in pain. I tried to push myself up, but gave up when I felt a stab in my stomach.

"Go home, Kay!" someone yelled from what must have been a window. "You're dirtying up our lawn!"

More laughs, louder this time. No offers to help, just tittering giggles from various windows. It was enough to motivate me to try getting up again. I pushed through the pain this time, dry heaving as I did so, but ended up on my knees as my reward for the exertion. The spray of sprinklers was now hitting me directly in the face, otherwise I may have never made it to my feet. I felt like I had been cut in half and only partially sewn back together.

Realizing by now where the pain was most concentrated, a new kind of tears pricked my eyes.

No, was all I could think. No, no, no! You're just overreacting. It's your imagination! But of course I knew in my heart that wasn't true. I needed to get home, but I could barely waddle, and with every step I could feel something leak out of my body. Blood was my only guess of what it could be, and I felt light-headed at the implications of what that meant. I tried to walk normally so I wouldn't have to feel myself falling apart, but the pain was too intense.

I sobbed then, leaning against a tree as I did so with the sprinklers doing their business as usual, as if I didn't even exist. Did my sorority sisters even know what happened? Would they be laughing like that if they did, or would one of them come help me?

The eight blocks to my apartment never seemed so far, but since it was going to hurt no matter how I got to it, I decided to run. Then, three steps later, when I felt something tear, I decided to run harder. I was wet and bleeding and the only sanctuary I had was closer with each step. I was close to passing out again, but it didn't matter. What was the worse that might happen? I'd wake up on someone else's front lawn?

The moment I reached my front door, I knew I was going to throw up. It was just a matter of whether I would make it to the toilet. By a miracle I did, hanging over the lid and sobbing uncontrollably as I let my body do its thing.

Luckily my roommate was MIA, which meant there was no one to answer to. No one to ask me what was wrong. No one to see me like this. No one to complain about the two hour bath I was about to take.

I flipped on the water in the bath and started to take off my clothes—or at least the ones I was still wearing. It hadn't taken me too long after waking up to figure out my bra was gone or that the shirt I was wearing wasn't mine. The pants and shoes were mine, though, for whatever good that was.

Flushing the toilet, I pushed myself up to my feet. I was too numb to care about the pain anymore, and more interested in whose shirt I was wearing. For the first time, I looked in the mirror and saw a pale rat girl with raccoon eyes. The mascara around my eyes had bled into dark circles with little black streams dripping down my face. My wet hair had plastered itself randomly to my head, and my skin was as pale as bone. My new shirt was whiter still and had been written on with a Sharpie.

THE GODS ARE APPEASED!

I stared at the writing, reflecting in reverse in the mirror, and knew exactly what had happened. And more than that, I knew that every girl who had been laughing at me that morning knew exactly what she was laughing at.

Me. Stupid, backward, gullible, Southern me!

I couldn't get the shirt off fast enough, tearing at it, wishing it would rip, before finally hurling it to the tile floor with a wet slap.

And then I could only stare in the mirror, seeing for the first time what my aching body looked like from the waist up. Slowly, I undid my pants, carefully peeling them from my body and gently stepping out of them.

Horror and humiliation washed over me as I realized how infinitely stupid I was and how much I deserved what I had gotten.

Stupid, stupid, stupid!

Hadn't Rhea tried to warn me? Hadn't she! From the day we did my makeover to making me promise not to take any drinks. Hadn't I sensed that the invite was too good to be true?

Yet I had ignored every little hint along the way.

A wave of exhaustion hit, and I knew if I didn't make it to my bed I would collapse where I stood. I willed my feet to move but when I felt the world go black, I didn't fight it. I bowed gratefully to the darkness and let it overtake me. Again.

* * *

Everything moved at a mad dash after that. Delivering the journal and having a bilingual officer flip through it to find where Julia Hernandez explained the situation and named her killer: Gabriel Wilson. Racing to the arrest site and preempting regularly scheduled programming as the twenty-seven-year-old killer was led to a police cruiser, then zipping back up the mountain for the ten o'clock news to report where dozens of police cruisers had come to search the cave.

The first five minutes of the night broadcast was all me and Dahl. And we had a lot to say about how a wife and mother had ended up dead in her own home. According to her own words, it had all begun with a visit from her brother. He hadn't stayed long, because his erratic behavior wasn't good for the children. So Julia and her husband had asked him to find somewhere else to stay. The next day, he disappeared, which was a relief until Gabriel Wilson showed up in his place and demanded payment for his drugs. Abel and Julia had no idea what he was talking about, but Gabriel insisted that they either tell him where the brother was or pay the money that was owed him. If they didn't, the kids might have an accident.

Julia searched for her brother everywhere, but there was no trace. Worse yet, Gabriel had started targeting her while she was alone, and she hadn't wanted to tell her husband that.

Gabriel was pushing harder and harder. She just wanted the situation to go away.

The plan had been to fake her death while hiking and then run back to Mexico until the policy paid out. What they would do from there wasn't solid, but the whole plan bought her time. The policy wouldn't become valid for at least ninety days after she created it, so Gabriel had to lay back for that long. Julia had planned on disappearing around the hundredth day, only to have Gabriel show up the first day possible and shoot her.

I wanted to put a picture of Julia's brother up right next to Gabriel's on the screen. The two deserved to share a cell at bare minimum. As a liberal, I had made it a stance to oppose the death penalty, but sometimes, in cases like this, I found myself slipping a bit.

"Crazy day," Nick said as we wrapped up.

"Yeah, I definitely owe you a drink," I said, turning off my mic. "You ran around like a champ today, Nick. How did it feel?"

"Insane," he said, pulling his camera from his tripod. "But amazing too. Time's never moved so fast."

He might just be cut out for success after all. I hadn't heard a peep of complaint about overtime, which was part of the reason for my good mood. Another reason for my good mood was walking my way in Circle S slacks.

We'd worked well together. Flawless, almost. Somewhere along the way, he'd decided to loosen up a little bit, and the result had been a perfect news night. Carla was going to kiss my feet. Angela would force herself to choke out a compliment. I wanted my raise, I wanted prime time, and I was going to get both.

I tucked my microphone away and offered him a smile. "Great job, officer."

He almost smiled back. "Can we talk?"

That sounded ominous. "Isn't that what we're doing right now?"

He motioned to a spot a little farther away. "Privately?"

The look in his eyes was hard to read, but I nodded and moved to the other side of the road with him. "What's up?"

He hesitated. "First off, congratulations on tonight. You really made it happen."

"Thanks," I said, knowing that was not why he sequestered me.

"It almost feels wrong that I had fun tonight, but it felt good to be so involved."

I wiggled my eyebrows at him. "We can try it again sometime."

That's when his mood changed. "Yeah, I don't think that's a good idea."

"Why not?"

"Because . . ." He hesitated, not looking at me at first, then looking again and looking away after briefly glancing at my lips. "I like you. I shouldn't, but I do. And I really want to kiss you right now, but we both know that's a dead end road."

To my surprise, his words actually hurt like a physical knife sliding in between my ribs and robbing me of my breath. It was a silly reaction, really, since I totally agreed with him. There was no future for us except for hours upon hours of ideological argument. But why did I get the sense that he was saying goodbye?

"I'm sorry for how rude I've been to you since you showed up. You really are a rare person. I didn't want to see it, but you are."

He was totally saying good-bye, and he couldn't be doing a worse job of it. If anything, he should be pissing me off, not rubbing my face in the fact that he was walking away to avoid liking me. That totally blew. The pinch in my chest tightened as I cinched up my guard.

"Are you blowing me off, Dahl? Is this your way of saying thanks for a fun night but you won't be calling back?"

"Yeah." His voice was so soft, I wanted to pretend I didn't hear it. "We both know that if I don't, a day is going to come soon where you're going to invite me back to your place, and I don't know if I'll be able to say no, Kathryn. When I'm with you, I forget what's important, and it's better if I just walk away now."

So now I was some temptress that would lure him into forsaking his religion? Okay, maybe I was. I didn't care one lick what he chose to believe about God. He could believe whatever he wanted, and unless it involved suicide bombing, I'd probably roll with it. I did want to touch him, though. I wanted him to prove that one stupid night years ago hadn't left me forever broken and that I could do what every other woman on the planet did without downing a quart of vodka first.

So, yeah, he'd read me right. I wanted to take him to a bed and test where my panic point with him was. Maybe not that night, but sometime.

"You deserve a good man, Kathryn. I'm not him. Before we both get confused about that, we should just walk away."

This shouldn't be hurting as bad as it did. We barely knew each other. We'd met less than five weeks ago. We'd spent less than two days together. Before my eyes watered up and gave me away, I stuck out my hand.

"Well, it was nice working with you while it lasted then."

Slowly, his hand reached for mine and shook it. "It really was."

"I'll miss you when you go to Church security."

"Yeah." Our hands held on. He wasn't pulling away, so I did.

"I'd say call me if you need anything, but we both know you won't." My voice sounded bitter, even to me.

"I'm sorry if I hurt you. And I'm sorry for kissing you up there. It sent mixed messages, but it proved how I can't say no to you. If Rhea hadn't shown up . . ."

"Nothing would have happened," I finished. "I wouldn't have ravished you. Promise."

"I know," he said quickly. "I know that, but . . ."

More than anything, I hated unfinished sentences. Especially from Dahl. "But what?"

"But nothing. Saying more doesn't help the situation. The point is that I'm not going to be alone with you again. And I'm going to avoid you, just like I did after Jackson Hole. Only better this time."

What could I say to that? "Well, at least I won't have to wonder."

"I figure I owe you that much. And in nine days I'll be completely off your radar. No harm, no foul."

"Sounds tidy," I said, trying for humor. It didn't work.

He backed away. "Again, great working with you, Miss McCoy."

"You too, Officer Dahl."

Then he turned and walked away. He just walked. Not one look back. Strangely hollow, I crossed back to the van.

THE PHONE RANG. Or at least I think it did. It didn't really matter. Then there was a knock on my door and voices. Two people. One swearing, the other silent. The first asking if the other heard water running and the other saying to check out the bathroom. A moment later, I felt something cover me. A blanket.

"It was the tub," the lower voice said a moment later. "She's lucky she didn't block the drain or this place would be flooded."

Strong hands gripped me through the blanket, lifting me and setting me on my bed.

There were whispers then, the door opened and shut, and I somehow knew one of them had left. Appreciating the warmth the blanket brought, I let everything go dark again.

* * *

The next morning I felt empty, which was stupid. But since when did feelings make sense? That didn't change the fact that I wanted them to makes sense.

There had to be a reason Dahl's rejection was hitting me so hard. I was probably just reacting to the fact that Dahl had rejected me before I could reject him. Hurt ego. That's all it was. Dahl and I weren't even friends. And when it came to qualities I was looking for in a man, he failed everything—

even the physical. I liked my men slender, corporate, and rich. Like Alan White. There was a man with flexible morals and no room to judge anything I did. And if for some reason Alan and I went fist to fist, I'd have a fighting chance.

That's what I looked for in a man.

Dahl's bulk could pin me against a wall one-handed, and I'd be helpless. He was totally blue collar and actually made less than me. A total deal-breaker was the fact that the man had never grown out of being a Boy Scout. With his idealistic morals and inflexibility, Dahl would never be more than what he was: a good soldier. But worst of all, was the whole religion thing. As if things weren't shaky enough with my family after I voted for Obama. If Mama ever—*ever*—caught wind that I was dating a Mormon . . . Well, I didn't even know how to finish that thought.

As far as pro-con lists went, there wasn't any upside to any kind of relationship with Dahl. I should be relieved that he didn't want to see me socially. One less man to worry about.

"Ready to roll," Nick said, pulling me back to the story at hand.

Should perpetrators of hate crimes be allowed to use facial makeup to cover hate-focused tattoos during a trial? Hear the judge's ruling at five. That's all I needed to say. Trouble was, I couldn't get my game face on. I didn't care—and I always cared!

"You okay?" Nick asked, his eyebrows knitting together adorably.

Why couldn't I like Nick? We got along. We had conversations and everything, but I wasn't attracted to him. I preferred him to other cameramen, but if Nick left me for greener pastures, I wouldn't go all catatonic and apathetic.

How could I feel so much loss with Dahl when we hadn't had anything to begin with? Well, other than a series of snarky, competitive conversations.

The upside to my freak funk was the fact that I could finally relate to how Rhea had fallen so hard and so fast for Ty. After three months of friendship and one month of dating, Ty had proposed. The insanity of that still boggled my mind, but my heart totally understood now. I could count the numbers of days I'd spent time with Dahl on one hand, and yet . . .

Yeah, Dahl's unfinished sentences were contagious because I didn't want to finish that thought either. But I understood Rhea's situation with Ty much better now. Utah must be some sort of freak vortex relationship catalyst. While the rest of the world took relationships at a natural and cautious pace, Utah propelled them forward, even when you were trying to stand still. Even when you backed away, you were still somehow moving forward—like some rogue moving sidewalk forever underfoot. It should come with a warning. "The moving sidewalk is for your mating convenience. Please stand to your right, so that others may be sucked past you at lightning speed on your left."

I'd spent too much time in airports.

"Kathryn?" It was Nick again. "We've got to get this promo. You ready?"

"Yeah."

If Rhea was feeling anything close to what I was feeling, she had to be in hell. She'd never imagined herself married. Not really. In her mind, it was a miracle on par of Ben reforming and turning into a monogamist. Possible, but not worth betting on. Then she'd met those stupid missionaries and made an idiotic promise that ultimately led her straight to Ty. Looking back, I could allow that it had all been fate. Under no other possible circumstances would she have met the only man on God's green earth that would make her believe such a thing as "happily ever after" could be a line in her personal history. And she was seriously thinking of walking away and going back to how things were.

She was about to pull a Dahl. I felt it in her. She was about to look Ty in the eye and explain to him why their relationship made no sense, and that they should both just cut their losses and move on. And Ty was going to feel a whole lot worse that I did.

In front of me, Nick was starting to look worried. I didn't blame him. But I also couldn't concentrate.

"Can you give me five?" I asked him. "I need to make a call."

"Sure. Yeah," he said while taking a look at his watch. We were behind schedule, but I didn't care as I put some distance between us and speed dialed a number that probably didn't deserve a shortcut anymore. I hadn't called Ben in at least a month. Things were weird now that he had a baby to play daddy to, but that didn't mean he got a pass on situations like this.

"Well, look who it is," he said, picking up.

"Hey," I said, glad he was in a good mood. "How's the biggest screw-up I know?"

"Screw-up?" he mocked. "I guess you haven't heard. The band's officially signed. Mercury Records, baby."

"I heard. And congrats." But we both knew that wasn't why I was calling. "How's your little princess?"

"You'd die if you saw her, Kate. She got all the good DNA."

"You need to post photos online so I can see. Your last ones are two months old."

"I know," he said. "Time just flies."

One more obligatory question remained to be asked before I could jump into the real reason of my call. I considered skimming over it, but it was better all around if I acknowledged the elephant in the room.

"And Cathy? How's that going?"

"Good," he said a little too quickly. "We're good right now, but you didn't call to talk about that."

"No," I agreed. "I didn't. I called because Rhea needs her best friend."

The other line of the phone went silent for a few seconds. "I'm not her best friend anymore."

"Fine. Her oldest friend, then," I amended. "Life's hitting her with both fists right now, Ben, and she needs someone who can see through her posturing."

"Are you saying you can't?" he asked, sounding agitated.

"No, I'm saying that I'm invested and biased, and she knows it. She needs someone to talk straight to her right now, and no matter what limbo you two are in, Rhea knows you want the world for her. She needs you, so if you still consider her your friend, you should call her."

"Call her?" he echoed, his voice about a half an octave higher than usual.

"That, or come out here and meet the guy she wants to marry. You have a gig tomorrow?"

"No. Did you say marry?" The word shook any trepidation he was having right out of him. "She's only been out there five months!"

A bitter laugh escaped me. "Welcome to Utah, Ben. I think there's something in the water here, if you want to know the truth, but that's off point. I'm calling you because Rhea needs you, not me, this time. Let me buy you a plane ticket to get you and Ty in the same room."

"Ty," he breathed, as if trying the word on for size. "Sounds preppy. And I don't need you to buy me a ticket."

"You're coming then?" My heart fluttered in hope, and only then did I realize that I'd missed Ben. In my own way, I might just need him as much as Rhea did.

"It's not that easy," he protested. "I have plans tomorrow."

"Worthwhile things are never easy, but you both need this. Cancel your plans. I've got to go, but Rhea needs to see you and Ty side by side. Then she needs to sit down alone with you and let you know what she's dealing with—and it's big, Ben. Freaky big. Crap you warned her about, so you're the perfect one to say 'I told you so.' Then everyone's going to have to make choices and live with them, so get your butt out here."

"You make it all sound quite dramatic," he said, although his voice was cautious.

"You'll have to let me know when you leave if you think I'm overstating," I said.

He hesitated. "It's not a good week—"

"You have an infant, Ben. No weekend is going to be a good weekend—not for eighteen years, so buck up and get out here." It worked to my favor that I didn't have time to wait for his response as I slid my phone shut.

The funk was gone. Ben was coming, which meant one good thing might come from the whole mess of my life. Knowing that put a gust of wind into my sails as I turned back to Nick.

"Let's do this," I said and turned on my mic.

FOURTEEN

THE NURSE LEFT the room, her face grave.

"What does it say?" I asked. Rhea didn't respond immediately.

"That you are a perfect candidate to press charges," she said, her face all business, but her voice catching in a way that let me know she was swallowing her own emotions. "That you were a virgin raped in multiple fashions by an undeterminable number of men and you lost a good amount of blood." She was quiet for a moment, then, "I am so sorry, Kay."

Tears stung my eyes. "Don't, Rhea. Just don't. You tried to tell me."

She shook her head. "They played me too. They knew exactly what would send me running. I knew something was up, though. I should have stayed."

I thought of Ben and Jasmine. If only I had told Rhea about the plot, things might have turned out differently. If anyone deserved blame for how the night turned out, it was definitely me. "I would have left too, Rhea. How were you supposed to know? I'm the one who didn't read the warning signs. I have no one to blame but myself."

"Don't you dare blame yourself!" she said with barely controlled rage. Then more softly, "Don't you dare. They chose you because of me, Kay. If I would never have talked to you this wouldn't have happened."

The nurse walked back in, which stopped me from saying anything back.

"Katie, we're all done here," the nurse said. "I'm just concerned at the extent of your injuries, and while the rape kit is no charge, I'm afraid I'll need your insurance information so we can take care of the other procedures."

My heart froze inside of me.

"Do you have insurance through your parents?"

No. They could not know about this. Ever.

Rhea cleared her throat. "She wouldn't let me bring her here unless I promised her family would never find out. She should have insurance through the school. That should take care of whatever she needs."

The nurse turned to me. "Did you get insurance through the school when you enrolled?"

"I—I don't think so. I didn't read anything about it."

"It's included," Rhea said confidently.

The nurse looked doubtful for a moment before a look of realization crossed her face. "Of course, you're right," she said, sharing a look with Rhea before turning and smiling to me. "Now if you'd get into this wheelchair for me, Katie, I'd like to wheel you in to meet one of our best doctors. He's going to fix you up."

"Where's the bathroom?" Rhea asked out of the blue.

"To your right and at the end of the hall," the nurse said brightly.

"Don't leave," I pled, not knowing if I could go through more probing without some moral support.

"I'll only be a minute," she said easily. "I'll be there in time for your consult. Don't worry."

We were separated then, me being wheeled down the hall while Rhea went the other direction. Minutes passed. Five and then ten, and I was so relieved to see Rhea walk through the door to join me that I didn't find it at all odd that she came in right behind my new doctor.

* * *

Friday. Rhea and I were supposed to go horseback riding after work. We would have if I hadn't made a stupid decision. Alan White called again about the fund raiser that night. He hadn't asked anyone else. Would I go?

He was my type, and I was his. More than that, he wasn't terrified by the fact he was attracted to me. There was every reason to say yes, so I did. Screw the vortex of mismatched relationships! I was going to go out with a man I could actually foresee a relationship with.

Take that, universe.

"You should come," I told Rhea over the phone. "Bring Ty. You two need a date, and you both like art. It'll be good to see what the scene's like here."

Rhea hesitated. "Do you happen to look at what it's raising money for?"

That was a weird question from her. "No. Does it matter?"

"To me? No. But you might run into someone there that you'd rather not. It's raising money to donate to college scholarships for kids who have lost a parent in the Iraq war."

A war that Dahl had done three tours of duty in before becoming a cop. Perfect.

"The guy makes less than I do. What are the chances he's even going to show up to something like this? He can't afford anything."

"Just a warning," Rhea said in her Switzerland tone.

"Not worried about it," I said as another call rang in. It was Ben. "Rhea, I need to go, but come. How often are their excuses to dress up in this state?"

"I'll ask Ty."

"Great. I have another call."

"Take it."

"Bye." I clicked over to Ben. "When do I pick you up?"

"Oh, so you just assume I'm coming?"

"Yes. What time?"

"One-thirty. Tomorrow," he said, sounding all moody. Ben could be worse than a girl sometimes. "I'm coming in on Delta."

"They have a pick-up zone here. You'll see it right past the taxis. I'll pick you up there."

"Fine. I've got to go now. We're playing tonight."

"Knock 'em dead."

"Will do."

His call was almost enough to put me in a good mood. In less than twenty-four hours, I was going to have some Ben time. And if there was anyone on the planet who could create a laundry list of reasons as to why I shouldn't be interested in Dahl, it was Ben.

And in the meantime, I had a date with a filthy rich lawyer. It was kind of hard to throw a pity party over that.

MY FIRST DAY *back at classes was horrific. I don't know how, but somehow I had gotten the idea into my head that what happened could be my little secret.*

It wasn't. Apparently everyone knew, and they didn't make a secret out of it. The whispers, looks, and occasional laughs filled the first part of the day, but by the second half I had caught a whisper of what people were calling me now.

Special K—one of the many street names for ketamine. The thing that shocked me is that it was mostly girls who were doing the mocking. Girls who knew what happened—possibly helped stage it—were now laughing at me over it. It was too much, and by the time my fourth class came around there was nothing I wanted more than to go back to my apartment and sit in the dark.

I took the shuttle home since it still hurt to walk. I'd taken pain killers, but they had done little more than take off the edge. I sat alone on the bus with my face hanging in my hands so no one would see me crying. It was a small dignity after everything that had happened and I clung to it.

At least they wouldn't see me cry.

The shuttle dropped me off a half a block from my apartment and I limped the remaining distance to safety. There was no one on the street, so I let the tears stream openly.

I missed home. I missed Lady. I wanted to fall into Mama's arms and fall asleep knowing I was loved. She would be more than happy if I came home and called it quits. Jake and I would be married, and everything would be peachy keen.

A week ago that would have been a very real possibility, but somehow the past few days had turned it into a fantasy. There was no way I could marry Jake now. There was no way he would want me now. He would never forgive me for not being my first, and there was no way I was ever going to tell him what really happened.

It would be better if he thought I moved to California and became easy.

I was limping up the stairs when I smelled fresh paint, which was odd, considering how dilapidated my dorm building was. Nothing in it looked as if it had been painted in the last decade.

It shouldn't have taken me so long to catch on. I should have realized what was happening before I turned the corner to my apartment where I saw Rhea, Ben, and Isaac kneeling and standing in front of my door. They were painting the door furiously, trying to cover up a Special K logo that had been stenciled on it.

Isaac saw me first.

"Kay . . ." He didn't seem to know what to say beyond that. Ben and Rhea looked at me, their faces solemn. They exchanged the briefest of looks before Ben stood and approached me.

"Do you want to step outside with me, Kay?"

"Don't call me that!" I screamed, pointing at the stencil on my door. "Anything but that!"

"Okay," he agreed. "Katie? Kate?"

I didn't reply. I could only stare at my door until his arm gently linked into mine and turned me away from the scene.

"C'mon," he said. "I need some fresh air."

I followed him. It wasn't like I had a choice. To my surprise, he led me up the stairs rather than down.

"You okay, Katie? Does it hurt to go up stairs?"

I shrugged as if it didn't matter one way or the other, and the next moment he had me cradled into his arms as if I was a child.

"I got you. Just enjoy the ride."

It was too easy to hold onto him—to let my head cradle into the hollow of his neck and remind myself that there were still good men in the world. When we were at the top of the staircase by the roof hatch, Ben set me down gently.

"It's locked," I told him.

"I know," he replied and pulled out something that looked like a pocket knife. "Give me a second."

It was closer to ten, but I was still amazed when the lock popped open. He opened it and held it open to me.

"No one will bother us up here."

"Us?" I asked, unable to meet his eyes.

He shrugged, looking somewhat sheepish. "I'm here if you need me, but I can wait for you inside if you want me to."

I paused. Hesitant. Scared. "And what if I don't want that?"

"Then I'm here for whatever you need."

I didn't hesitate. If I stopped to think about it there was no way I would allow myself to do what I did next. And once again, I buried my face into Ben's chest, I didn't come up for air for quite some time.

* * *

I couldn't concentrate on the art. All my attention centered around Alan's hand resting on the small of my back. Guiding me. Steering me. Implying control. I thought I'd gotten past feeling like this with Dahl. But, no. When I stepped away, Alan nestled back in. And each time his hand found the small of my back again, the invisible band around my chest tightened.

The persistent touch was subconscious on his part. He might not even be aware he was doing it. But I was, and no matter how I tried, I couldn't ask him to stop. I didn't know how to without showing my agitation.

My hand reached out for my sixth courtesy glass of wine since we'd arrived. Alan's eyes narrowed as I sipped and tried to reach the point where possessive hands didn't feel like nails on a chalkboard. Griswolds weren't cheap drunks, but Alan didn't know that. He was probably wondering if I was about to get sloppy on him.

To give him some peace of mind, I pretended to consider the ridiculous piece of art in front of us. Someone had painted a canvas blue with a large yellow stripe off of center and a red blob in the bottom right corner. Looked like it took ten minutes of someone's time and they were trying to sell it for $2,500.

"You like it?" Alan asked from my right. I turned to look at him. Tall, slender, fit, and looking like a powerhouse in his charcoal Gucci two-button suit. He looked like he had just walked out of a magazine ad with his perfectly trimmed dark hair graying gracefully at the temples. I hadn't known him long enough to know whether his skin was tanned from an active lifestyle or from frequent visits to a tanning bed, but the contrast against his brilliant white teeth and sky blue eyes made him the picture of an attractive man.

Yet I wasn't attracted.

I felt his hand snake around my waist and hold. "It doesn't have a name. What would you call this piece?"

Using a sip to take a moment, I frantically tried to think of something intelligent to say. What would Rhea say? "Carpathia."

"Really?" his asked, his voice high with surprise. "I see it. Very dark."

"What would you call it?" I returned, hoping to avoid a follow-up question.

"Well, I had been thinking along some other lines, but I think I might call it Carpathia now as well."

The conversation was too lame to indulge, so I turned to the nude on the next wall. Men liked looking at nudes.

Alan's hand stayed around my waist as we moved to it. I took another sip of wine, hoping he wouldn't ask me what I would entitle a picture of a pear-shaped woman's backside. He didn't. Instead, he used the opportunity to step behind me and hold me from behind, one hand resting on each hip. To the outside eye the change made us appear like any number of other couples in the room, but it was the moment I knew his plans for the night ended with me at his place.

Slow down, buddy, I thought as Dahl arrived with a woman.

What were the chances?

Forgetting the pear-shaped backside, I sized up his date, trying not to laugh openly at her wardrobe choice for the evening. It covered so much skin that it made the Amish look immodest, and if she even dabbed an ounce of make-up on her face I couldn't see it from where I was standing.

Homely. Textbook homely, that's what she was, and Dahl was sending her his most relaxed, perfect smile.

I drained my glass.

Why was Rhea always right? Always. It was nauseating sometimes, but I chose not to be unhappy about the situation. It would be good for him to see me with Alan so he knew I had plenty of options—options who knew how to dress and treat a lady. But even as I admired Gucci, I found myself looking over Dahl's ensemble—it was the same one he'd worn for his interview with me a few days before. Did he own anything else? Had he even washed it? I should go over and give it a sniff and check.

It was that thought that clued me into the fact I was tipsy. There would be no sniffing Dahl's clothes over the course of the evening.

I leaned into Alan in an unspoken rebellion. Sure, his touch grated, but no more than the knowledge that I was likely only attracted to Dahl because he reminded me of what I grew up with. I'd decided over the course of the day that was the most logical explanation for by abrupt attraction to him. Dahl was like my dad in so many ways, but I'd already chosen the trajectory of my life. Up, not back. Alan, not Dahl . . . or some version of Alan, at least. Maybe a version that wasn't so grabby.

A waiter walked by, and I grabbed another glass of wine, depositing my old glass on the tray. This time around, the wine was a Zinfandel. I was mixing colors and didn't care. All I needed was to get buzzed enough to take the tension out of my back and ignore the cramp developing in my abdomen.

"You're thirsty tonight," Alan said in my ear.

I let out a laugh. The sound was a little too hearty to be ladylike. "I haven't had a drink in months. I think I'm just compensating."

His hand tightened on my waist. "Then I'll make it my responsibility to make sure you get home safe and sound."

I angled my head back to him to shoot him a crooked smile, and he dropped a kiss on the side on my neck.

"Excuse me," Rhea's voice said from out of nowhere. She must have teleported in because I didn't see her arrive. Bibbity bobbity boo! That was Rhea for you. "Can I steal Kathryn for a moment, Alan?"

"Of course," Alan said, finally dropping his hands. At last, no heat spots burning their way through my clothes. Rhea hooked my arm and led me away.

"Let me take you home," she said.

"So early?" I complained. "You just got here. Where's Ty?"

"We've been here a while," she said, pointing him out. I sent him a pinky wave, which he did not return.

"Grumpy," I accused, even though he couldn't hear me.

"Ty's worried that you're planning to sleep with this guy," she said, facing off with me. "And we both know he's right."

"And? Who's going to stop me?" Not Rhea. She'd promised to stay out my business when it came to that, and she always kept her word. Always. Just like Dahl, the big Boy Scout who dreamed of taking a bullet for the Mormon prophet. He probably thought his life sure would mean something then—that his ex-wife would sob buckets for leaving him and every wrong thing he'd ever done in his life would somehow be made right.

I glared at him and his homely date from across the room.

"Kay—" Rhea pled.

"How many times do you think that dress has been washed?" I asked, talking over her. "Seriously, could that hem be any more curled? You'd think Suzy Homemaker would own an iron."

She chose to ignore the comment. "Kay, we both know why you choose to get drunk. Let me take you home so you can get a re-do on this whole situation."

"Who's the woman with Dahl?" I asked instead of responding to her point.

"It's—"

"Never mind. I don't care. If he wants to date women with wide birthing hips, that's his business."

Rhea's jaw flexed as she fought the urge to respond, and she glanced at Ty, who was standing at the entrance, looking worried. If it hadn't required crossing a room, I would have hugged the guy. He always had my back. Just like one of my brothers.

I needed another drink.

"Let us take you home," she pressed again. "As your friend, I can't watch you do this."

For some reason that made me laugh. "But you have to. You promised, remember?" I snickered again. "It's just sex, Rhea. You should try it sometime."

I expected a reaction. A flinch or ideally a slap. Something to get her out of my face. She didn't want to see me like this, and I didn't want to be seen, so why was she still talking to me? Why was she stepping in closer.

"See that guy over there?" she said softly, obviously referring to Ty.

"Duh."

"Some things are worth waiting for, Kay," and she left it at that. No preaching, that wasn't her way. No advice either. Just a simple statement capable of making me feel like utter crap.

"I'll let you know when I find something like that," I shot back at her.

Her face stayed impassive until she gave a few quick blinks. Tears? Not possible. "Fine. Call me if you need a ride home. I'll come get you, okay?"

"Yes, Mom."

Finally I'd succeeded in stinging her. I saw it as she backed away, leaving me to face the night alone like a big girl. I wanted to run after her, but I didn't. I walked back to Alan and let him drop another kiss on my neck.

"You smell amazing," he whispered in my ear while we both watched Rhea and Ty leave. Alan had probably listened in on the whole conversation.

"Thanks."

His hands found my waist again and I refused to care. "I want you to pick something out for my office."

"We'll find something perfect," I promised as I laced my fingers through his and led him to the next piece.

The next twenty minutes and four drinks were a blur, but they ended up in front of the Icarus marked "SOLD." I stared at it, tears coming to my eyes for some inexplicable reason.

"Are you okay?" Alan asked gently in my ear.

"It's beautiful," was all I could say.

He moved closer to look for the price. "It says it's already been sold."

"Yeah, I know."

"If you want, I could try to outbid the previous buyer."

For some reason that brought a smile to my lips. "And have

a naked male statue in your office?"

"I'd buy him for you, not me. But you still haven't picked out something for my office."

"Well, that depends on the color palette of your office," I said. "I cannot make a suggestion without a mental image of where the picture will hang."

"Well, there's a lot of mahogany," he explained, his eyes dropping to my lips. "And depending what room you're in, the carpet is either taupe or emerald green."

"Your office is green," I decided.

"What makes you say that?" He was standing too close.

"You strike me as a green fan," I said, surveying the gallery from a distance and purposefully ignoring his question. What kind of man let a drunk woman pick his office furnishings? And where was Dahl?

My eyes scanned, looking for an oversized Mattel doll, and came up empty. Then again, if I'd had eyes in the back my head, I wouldn't have nearly jumped out of my skin when Dahl's deep voice greeted me from behind with a simple, "Kathryn."

His tone was clipped and when I turned to face him I saw his eyes matched the severe tone of his voice. I said nothing in return, just returned his gaze before looking down at his date—hating her cow brown eyes, hound dog cheeks, and the hideous bargain-basement dress she was wearing that was even more appalling up close.

"Dahl, good to see you," I said brightly. "Here to support your comrades?"

He stiffened. "Of course."

"Huh. Too bad you can't afford anything."

His nose wrinkled as he caught the smell of alcohol on me. "I wanted you to meet my sister, but if I had known you were drunk I would have waited for a better time."

Sister? He had brought his sister to the fund-raiser?

"Good to meet you," she said with more enthusiasm than

could ever be authentic as she babbled. "You're dress is beautiful. The closest I've come to a dress that nice is panting on a display window." She cast a self-conscious look around. "I feel so out of place here, but Ken made me come anyway since I don't get out much. I've got five kids that really keep me busy, so it feels strange to be with so many quiet adults. Strange, but nice."

After about a half a second of lag time, I caught up with her spray of words.

"Five?" I couldn't help but gawk. "But you look like you're twenty-five."

Her eyes, which were now more like chocolate than cow brown, twinkled with a humor I didn't share. "Twenty-six, but who's counting anymore?"

In another life I could have been her, I realized—married with as many kids, all working a farm in southern Alabama. The thought had me feeling hollow, and it was several seconds before I remembered that I had someone to introduce too.

"This is Alan," I said quickly. "He's a successful attorney here in town. Alan this is Ken Dahl. He's an officer for the Salt Lake Police Department, and this is his sister . . ." I looked at her, drawing a blank. "I'm sorry, I didn't get your name."

"Barb," she said with a kind smile, and all I could think was, *No, they didn't!* What kind of parents named their children Barb and Ken when they had the last name of Dahl? Luckily for Barb, she'd gotten married young, but school must have been a nightmare.

Alan held out his hand, shaking both Dahl's and his sister's hands in turn. "Kathryn was just helping me pick out something for my office."

"I see," Dahl said, and I could feel his eyes on me. What was he going to do? Arrest me for public intoxication? He'd be right to do it, because the whole world seemed to be tilting slightly to the right. I took a steadying breath.

"Well, it's all for a good cause," Alan's voice was saying,

although it suddenly sounded far away.

"That, it is," was Dahl's reply. His sister was looking at me—the twenty-six-year-old mother of five who had probably never had a drink in her life. Well, hooray for her.

A picture caught my eye, looking fabulously 3-D in the fray of artlessness surrounding it. Circles and squares and shapes of every kind leapt from the canvas in a way I hadn't noticed the first time around.

"That one," I said to Alan, out of the blue. "With the gold frame."

"The one that looks like an engine?"

"Beautiful," I murmured.

His eyebrows furrowed, not initially pleased with my choice, but then he shrugged his shoulders. "Worth looking into, at least. Mind if I leave you with your friends for a moment?"

"Not at all," I said with a wave, realizing that had been my plan all along. I just hadn't caught on to myself in my tipsy state. The moment Alan was gone, Dahl's hand gripped my arm like a vice. My chest didn't clamp, my stomach didn't cramp, but my heart did pound as I licked my lips.

"What's going on?"

I tugged away from him. "Nothing. Let go."

He did, which totally annoyed me. He'd be easier to hate if he didn't respect my wishes. "You need a ride home."

"Alan will give me one."

"Yeah, I'll bet he will," Dahl snapped, his voice heavy with meaning. I ignored it and turned to his sister.

"Do you like art, Barb?" She had been watching us, and the question caught her off-guard.

"As much as the next person, I guess, although I could never afford any of this."

I gave a quick laugh. "Would you ever want to?"

She blinked in surprise. "I beg your pardon?"

"I asked if you would ever want to buy any of this crap? Your kids could probably do better than half of this."

A sly look came into her eye as her lips curved up. "I was actually thinking that myself a few minutes ago. Glad to hear an educated person agrees with me."

"Educated?" I echoed, amused by the term.

"Well, I assume you've been to a few of these."

"Too many," I agreed. "There's only one piece in here worth looking at." I gestured to the Icarus. "I'm pretty sure my friend bought it." I had been hoping that pointing out the statue would get Dahl to stop looking at me like he was about to handcuff me, but it didn't. He kept drilling his laser beam eyes into the side of my head as if daring me to turn away from his sister and face off with him.

If that's what he wanted, then it was the last thing I was going to give him.

Barb was saying something, and the whole world was still tilting to the right. That last drink was starting to hit my system and balance was becoming an issue. Not a major one, but enough to make me self-conscious in front of a cop.

While contemplating the affects of a public intoxication charge on my career, a pair of hands found my hips and smooth lips pressed against my shoulder.

"It's done," Alan said. "They deliver it to my office on Monday."

"Really?" I asked with more enthusiasm than was probably warranted. "Are you sure that's the one you wanted?"

"You chose it," he said, spinning me in his arms, and my heart shot into my throat when I realized he was going to kiss me right in front of Dahl and his sister. After an initial flinch, I decided to make show out of it, and when Alan pulled away he had the look in his eyes that every woman knows on sight.

"If you'll excuse us," he said to Dahl and Barb, "I think we're ready to go."

"Good to meet you," Barb said, while her brother stayed conspicuously silent.

"You ready?" Alan asked me. I tried for a sophisticated smile, but couldn't tell whether or not I succeeded in pulling it off, only that Dahl was walking away from me and his sister followed looking somewhat confused. I watched them go, and hated that he hadn't said a word—hadn't stepped in.

He really was stepping out of my life.

"Totally," I said and let him escort me to the door.

I *DIDN'T TELL ANYONE when I left. Not my teachers, not Rhea, not anyone. I just used my new credit card to take a taxi to the airport. I didn't pay attention to ticket price. I just needed out, and if I never saw another palm tree again in my life, it would be no loss to me.*

I spoke to no one on the two flights, and Jake picked me up at the airport. It was stupid not to call my parents, but I just didn't know what to say to them. Jake was easier. Less questions. More enthusiasm. Plus I'd promised I would call him first when I left.

He carried my bags for me, his blue eyes twinkling from under his cowboy hat and I found myself looking at him differently than I ever had before—like he was an object. A thing I could use— something I needed to use to get my feet back under me.

"You're quiet," he said when we were about halfway home. He couldn't seem to take his eyes off my hair.

"Just thinking about you," I replied, channeling the coy tone California girls used. "You wanna go out tomorrow night?"

"Tomorrow? Well, uh—"

"Whatever date you've got, break it," I said in a voice that conveyed more control than I felt. "I'll make it worth your while."

His eyes snapped to mine in an unspoken question.

I offered him a confirming smile. "Like I said: break the date."

* * *

Alan's bathroom was four-hundred square feet of luxury. It was bigger than my entire dorm room had been in college, and all I could do was bawl against the cheapest fixture in it. A look at my watch showed me that it had been only thirty seconds since the last time I checked the time.

I had to go. Whether Alan was asleep or not, I couldn't spend two more minutes in his place.

I stood up, looking at my pathetic face in the mirror and turning the faucet on to a trickle so I could clean up a bit. When I looked as good as I was going to get while sporting puffy eyes and a runny nose, I stood staring, wondering whether to call a taxi or Rhea. If I called a taxi, I wouldn't have to look Rhea in the eye, but if a taxi driver gave me so much as look over I probably wouldn't get into his car.

Part of me was mad at Rhea for not stopping me. She always swooped in and saved me. Not tonight, though. Tonight she had honored my wishes. I wanted to hate her for that. I wanted to hate her for any reason at all.

A taxi. I was definitely calling a taxi. I flipped my phone open, ready to dial when I saw a text from Rhea.

I'm one house over parked on the street. Come out when you're ready.

I started crying again. She had been out there the whole time, no doubt. Patiently waiting for me to come to my senses.

Taxi forgotten, I shoved the phone back into my purse and slipped from the bathroom past the now-snoring Alan. My footsteps were silent on his luxurious rugs as I let myself out, careful to lock his door behind me as I did so.

Rhea was right where she said she would be, her silver Audi gleaming in the moonlight. She didn't say a thing as I let myself in the passenger door. She simply closed her laptop. We sat in silence for a moment. I certainly didn't know what to say, so I was glad when she broke the silence.

"You want me to take you home?"

I didn't mean to cry. I meant to give her a simple yes and avoid making eye contact with her the rest of the ride home.

"It's like I'm in love with him," I heard myself whispering through tears instead. I'd never been in love, so I had no idea what I was talking about. It made no sense that I would be in love with Dahl. None. And the feeling couldn't be real or lasting. How could it be?

"I know," was her simple reply. So quiet, so confident. It was like she had known from the beginning that I would fall for Dahl with the same ease and clarity she foreseen me needing a ride home that night.

With a flick of Rhea's wrist, her car purred to life on the silent street and she pointed it toward home.

"Will you stay at my place tonight?" I hated myself for asking, but I couldn't help myself. I didn't want to wake up alone.

"Not a problem," she agreed and left me to my thoughts.

SEVENTEEN

*G***ETTING JAKE INTO** *the back of his pickup was easy. From there I just had to close my eyes and remember to breathe. My body still hurt, but I kind of liked the sting. It gave me an excuse to stay distant from everything that was happening.*

I should have accepted the drinks Jake offered me earlier. Not that beer came close to getting me drunk, but it could have helped. I'd have to try a few drinks next time, because everywhere Jake touched tension built until it cramped. It was supposed to feel good. Every book, every movie, every TV show, every conversation I'd ever had told me that having a guy kiss my neck was supposed to feel good. So why did I feel nothing, as if my mind were ignoring those nerves entirely?

"Breathe," I whispered to myself and hoped Jake didn't hear.

"You're even more beautiful than I imagined," he purred, kissing a trail along my neck, and I nearly cried then and there. Swallowing back the tears, I coached myself to stay focused until something smacked against the side of the truck. Hard.

"Get out!" a voice barked, and Jake leapt to his feet—not exactly covered. I reached blindly for something to cover my body before realizing who had caught us.

"Rhea?" I asked in shock.

She threw a wad of fabric at Jake. "Here's your clothes. Get dressed."

"Beggin' your pardon, ma'am," Jake said, covering himself, "but I don't believe that's your call. Katie and I are just fine, aren't we?"

"What in heaven's name are you doing here, Rhea?" was all I could say.

She responded by physically pulling me out of the truck bed. "Go, Jake. I've got a car here and will make sure Katie gets home just fine."

I thought Jake might argue with her, but something about her frosty eyes and the way she threatened him had him backing down.

"Something happened," he said, eyes lowered. It wasn't a question. He hopped over the truck bed and put on his shirt, looking at me with sad eyes. "I was hoping you came home because you loved me, but you didn't, did you?"

I couldn't say anything. I couldn't even look at him.

"Whoa," he breathed. "Okay, then." He tugged his jeans on, then his boots. "I'll turn my back while you dress."

Rhea studied Jake, clearly surprised by his sudden manners before handing me my clothes. When had she found the time to fold them? How long had she been there?

It didn't matter, I decided. I would never get over the humiliation whether she had been standing there for five seconds or five minutes. But now that she was there, it was best for Jake to leave. It was best he not hear anything I had to say.

"Get dressed," she said quietly and, with tears streaming down my cheeks, I did so.

"The car's just over here," she said when I was finished.

I nodded, and we started the trek in silence. Behind us, I heard Jake's truck start and pull away back toward town and felt the reality set in of how badly this would hurt him. I'd known Jake my whole life and now nothing would be the same between us ever again.

"Nice guy," Rhea said.

"You had no right to do that!" I screamed, getting right up

into her face. The fury I felt at myself was easy to redirect. "If I decide I want to sleep with someone, you have no right to interfere! Understand?"

"Okay," she said, keeping her voice even. "I promise I'll never stop you like this again, but I won't apologize for doing it now, so don't even ask."

She turned and started toward her rental car again. Not knowing what else to do, I followed. We were ten miles outside of town, and it would be insanity to walk.

"You can't run, you know," she said out of the blue. "I know you came home to run away from what happened, but it followed you here. Can't you see that?"

Tears fell at the truth of her statement, and suddenly I didn't want to get in her car. Instead, I sat down right in the dirt and cried into my Wranglers.

"It's okay," Rhea said, sitting down next to me. "Let it out."

Boy, did I! I cried one of those ugly cries, where something streams out of every part of your face, and when I heard fabric tearing and realized Rhea was ripping off part of her shirt for me to use as I tissue, I started crying harder. She handed the cloth to me.

"I'm sorry," she whispered. "I shouldn't have left you that night."

I shook my head. We'd been over this, but it seemed we both needed to say the words again. "You couldn't have known."

"But I did," she whispered. "I suspected it from the moment you got your bid."

The tears screeched to a halt, and I suddenly felt the heat of anger in my heart. "How? I knew you were never happy about me pledging, but how could you have known?"

I could see her mind work to avoid the question, but then she settled on dealing with it.

"They were nice." She said it as if that explained everything.

The flame of anger grew. "Not everyone who's nice is out to get you, Rhea."

"People are nice when they want something, Kay. At least they are where I come from. That's why you stick out. Anyone can see right off that you are too kind-hearted to be one of them. They're a cliquey bunch of spoiled kids whose parents are metropolitan multi-millionaires. That's what they're looking for when they look for pledges."

"I knew that," I confessed. "I sensed something was off but didn't care. I wanted to be good enough to hang out with your friends."

"First of all," Rhea said, holding up a finger, "they are not my friends! Never have been. Number two, you are way too good for them. And three, one of the main reasons they hate you is because you are more beautiful naturally than any of them will be with all their millions. All that crap they fed you about what to do to make yourself more attractive was advice to bring you down to their level. Forget it this instant if you know what's good for you!"

For some reason her words made me start crying again—crying because I had doubted the only person really looking out for me in L.A. And now she had flown all the way to Alabama to do the same.

Why? And how had she known where I lived or how to find me?

The question had to be asked.

"How did you find me? How did you get here so fast?"

She hesitated, debating her answer before she spoke. "Remember that Elliott Church guy?"

I nodded, knowing what was coming.

"I've started working for him." Then she smiled—actually smiled. "The man has amazing resources."

"I guess," I said as she offered me a hand up.

"Come on. Let's get you home to your parents."

* * *

I almost wished I had a hangover the next morning, but

being the descendent of generations of gin makers had endowed me with a cast-iron stomach. Not even a trace of a headache blurred the clarity of the previous night's events in my mind. I saw every moment as clear as day. I didn't have work to distract me either, since it was Saturday.

In lieu of staring at a wall, I stole one of Rhea's running routes—one of the ones she uses when she wants to feel her heart beat in her brain. It goes up past the State Capitol, past a place called Memory Grove, and up to a hiking trail that leads to the place where Brigham Young scoped out the valley when the Mormons first arrived. It's not a long route, but it's all uphill, and the last half mile is a dirt trail up a foothill.

The view from the top was soothing. It felt good to feel small—to see evidence of millions of lives beneath me—all with their own problems. It was an unexpected balm. I started watching the airport. In only a few short hours, Ben would be landing, which was perfect since I needed a hug in the worst way, and Ben was one of the guys I didn't flip out around.

He couldn't arrive soon enough for my taste.

Feeling better even though not a single thing had been resolved, I started down the mountain and back to my place. It would be a good day. Rhea was always helping me out, and today I was returning the favor with Ben. She missed him. She needed him. For over fifteen years he'd been her confidante. He knew her in a way that even I didn't. Jerk that he could be, she needed him.

I'd told her that morning I'd be by her place around two and that I needed to see her. She didn't know why, but I was certain she would be pleasantly surprised. In two hours, at least one of us would be happier.

Sprinting down the steep hills, I enjoyed the pain and burn of pushing myself hard. It felt cleansing, like some of the filth that had built up in me over the years might get squeezed out in the process. This was the high Rhea chased. I knew it. When life was hard and she went running, this was the clarity she was looking for. I should join her some time, but running with Rhea was like jogging with a bullet.

Zipping down State Street, I hit my zone, and I felt like I could go forever and not even need a drink of water. That was it. I was going to start training with Rhea. She had her own reasons for being fit, but I just wanted the high. This high. The clarity. A high that was being interrupted by cop lights flashing as a cruiser made a right hand turn in front of me and stopped to block the sidewalk.

Dahl stepped out in full uniform. So much for my Zen moment.

It was tempting to just run past him, but he was clearly intent on having me stop, so I slowed and said good-bye to my moment of perfection.

"What?" I said when I was reached his car.

His eyes leveled on mine. "What in the world happened last night?"

"Uh-uh," I said, moving to the crosswalk. "You don't get to have this conversation with me. In fact, I distinctly recall you saying you were going to avoid me. So far, you suck." He grabbed my arm, and I yanked away. "I believe touching was off limits too."

"I keep going over it in my mind, and it's like some bad dream. I stopped by your place to check on you. There was no answer."

He'd come by? Hearing him confess that had a pressure squeezing my throat, cutting off my air and making me feel light-headed, even as I shrugged nonchalantly. I wasn't playing that game with him anymore.

"That's probably because I wasn't home." I felt a sense of release confessing it, as if a burden were being lifted off my shoulders.

His voice was one of controlled rage. "You went home with

him?" He stepped in closer. "You slept with him?"

I gave him a blasé look, obeying my mind as my heart hammered its objection. "I wouldn't exactly call it sleeping, no."

I had no time to react. I don't know what I would have done if I had. As it was, I barely had time to shield my face from any potential shards of glass as Dahl punched his fist through his patrol car's side window. I stared for a moment, shocked at his sudden burst of violence and finding myself wanting to reach out and touch him, apologize to him, to stabilize him. But by doing that, I would expose myself, and there was no way I was ready for that again. There was no way I was going to let him make me feel worse than I already did by justifying his anger.

Instead, I leveled a hard look at him. "Tax dollars well spent. Or are you going to put that on your personal insurance?"

His eyes glared at me, wounded. "How can you be so cold?"

"Me?" I shot back, backing away. "Cold? Buddy, all I did was lower my temperature to match yours. You've got no one but yourself to blame for that."

He reached out and placed both his hands on his car, leaning on them for support as his head hung down to look at the ground. "I can't believe you slept with him."

My heart hurt. Impossibly so. Air didn't come easily, and my stomach churned in such a way I thought it might never feel right again. "You pushed me away," I whispered. "And I went." I took a stabilizing breath. "You should be pleased."

Not allowing time for a response, I crossed through the traffic and ran the rest of the way home. And damn him, Dahl let me.

EIGHTEEN

IT DIDN'T OCCUR to me that Mama would think Rhea looked like a terrorist. Nor did I remember that the anniversary of 9/11 was three days away when we walked into my parent's home. Whoops. As they'd say in Hollywood: My bad.

Luckily for me, Rhea politely stepped out of the house when evicted. Then Mama screamed to high heaven for twenty minutes before sending me to my room.

It was just how I left it, which, of course, made me cry again. I honestly didn't know where all the water was coming from. It wasn't until I heard my mother's raised voice that I realized my parents had brought Rhea back into the house.

Sneaking down the stairs, I flinched as the words got clearer. I owed Rhea more than I could ever repay and yet I couldn't walk into the den and tell Mama that Rhea was the best friend I'd ever had. But if I did that, my parents would force me to explain to them why she'd come at all. And they'd know if I lied.

I couldn't tell them. I couldn't look either of them in the eye and let them know how badly I'd screwed up. So instead of saving Rhea, I sat against the wall outside the den and listened to a hate storm.

"What did you do to her?" Mama screamed. "Is something so wrong with her hair and her face that they need to be covered up with chemicals?"

"No, ma'am."

"It makes me ill to know my daughter has been out there in your city of sin—"

"Mrs. Griswold, stop," Rhea snapped, her steady voice somehow cutting my mother off. "Do not pretend to know what I do and do not understand or delude yourself that you have any right whatsoever to speak to me this way." Whoa. I think I was as stunned as Mama as I waited for her to finish. "Your daughter needs you, ma'am. Why do you think she came home? Have you even talked to her to find out why?"

"Clearly, she came to her senses," Mama huffed. Daddy said nothing, and even though I didn't know Rhea that well, I could imagine the killer look in her eye as she stared them down. Daddy would respect her strength and clarity and understand why we were friends. I had to believe that. Oddly enough, while I was thinking about my dad, she addressed him.

"Do you believe that, Mr. Griswold?" she asked, her voice full of meaning. "Is your daughter one to give up easily and run home when things get hard?"

Her words cut deep because I knew my daddy would believe her. I didn't run from anything. Never had. Once I set my mind to something I had to be the best. Had to be. And I'd run. Mama wouldn't care about the thought process that sent me home, but my daddy would. How had Rhea picked up on that? Mama cared about the neighbors and appearances. Nothing would make her happier than my returning home, marrying Jake Eatonton, and living a few miles down the road as I brought grandchildren into her life.

Kids. Just the mere thought made it hard to breathe. I was eighteen. I knew girls my age who were excited to be moms, but I just felt so unprepared. What did I have to teach a kid except a bunch of theories my parents had told me that I'd never even really tried out?

I couldn't stay. The realization hit me so hard that Rhea's next words took a second to register.

"I don't care an inch what either of you thinks of me. You could not hate me more than I hate you right now for cutting your daughter off for moving to a city you knew she was unprepared to deal with." I heard a few steps, and Rhea's voice dropped. "You should have been on the phone with her every day, helping her—coaching her! Hearing what she had to say and helping her make sense of everything. She needed someone she knows and trusts holding her hand."

Never in my life had I heard anyone talk to my parents this way. Especially daddy. Women on the gossip circuit could be brutal, but they reserved talk like this for backstabbing. What was happening on the other side of the wall terrified me, even as Rhea's words ripped more tears out of me. I wanted to stomp my feet and scream that she was right! One of the many reasons I wasn't ready to become a parent myself was because I still needed my own parents.

A few more hushed footsteps drew my attention back into the other room, and I knew that the rubber-soled shoes belonged to Rhea. "You left your naïve daughter in the hands of strangers, Mr. Griswold. Think about it for two seconds: You left your beautiful, well-meaning, innocent daughter without money, family, friends, or even a telephone, alone in a city that values none of the things you love most about her." Rhea's voice cracked. "What do you think they did to her?"

The wall I leaned against shook as a vase smashed into it on the other side.

"Get out!" Daddy screamed. Never in my life had I heard him yell. Ever. And whichever vase he had thrown was worth a fortune. Everything in the front room was an heirloom.

"Gladly," Rhea said in an even voice, completely calm. "But I'm here to offer your daughter a choice. If she heads back with me, I'll be the one looking out for her. She'll have what she needs to succeed, with or without your support. Your family may have clout here, but you're paupers in my world. For your sake, though, *why don't you sit down with your daughter for five minutes and hear what she has to say? Then why don't you get over yourselves and support her?"*

Those were the last words out of her mouth before she moved from the living room to the hall leading to the front door—which happened to be just where I was sitting. She paused, her eyes unreadable as she regarded me on the floor. For a moment neither of us said anything as Mama screamed at my daddy in the other room about how Rhea was never allowed in our home again.

"I meant every word," Rhea said, her voice soft so it wouldn't be heard by anyone but me. "Whatever you choose is up to you, but if you come back to school, I've got you covered."

Then she was gone.

* * *

I turned the last corner to Rhea's home, my car slowing notably because of the hunk of a man in my passenger seat. Ben was a whole lot of tomcat for a little hybrid, but both of us were pretending not to notice.

He noted the mature trees and old, manicured homes and gave a little grunt of approval. "I can see her hiding out here."

"Yeah, you'll like her place," I agreed, sneaking him a glance. It seemed ages since I'd seen Ben, and he looked even better than I remembered. He looked like the rock star he was slowly becoming, with rangy muscles and the careful nonchalance of his wardrobe. Ben was completely memorable while always appearing haphazard. Rhea was a sucker for the look, and dropping Ben off on her front porch was tantamount to walking up and punching her in the gut.

Oh well.

Everyone needed a little kick to get them in the right direction. Even Ben. Maybe this answer wasn't perfect, but it was pretty close.

"Her boyfriend going to be there?" Ben asked.

I glanced at the clock in the dash and hoped that was the case. "He got off about an hour ago, so it's likely."

"You didn't tell him either?" Ben asked, laughing. "You always have liked to play with fire."

"Whatever," I grumbled. "You'll all thank me later."

"Oh, I'll thank you in advance. I want to see this little poser who thinks he's good enough for my Rhea."

My Rhea? I sent him a sidelong grin, which was meant to be playful. I didn't expect Ben's eyes to narrow in and assess me.

"And speaking of the girl who plays with fire, have you been burned recently?" His strong hands came up to cradle my chin so he could look into my eyes. I turned back to look at the road. Only three more driveways until Rhea's.

"What's his name?" Ben asked. "Want me to pay him a visit?"

"No," I said quickly. "That's not why you're here."

"I can pull double duty," he said, dropping his hand as I signaled to flip around and park on the street. "I might want to hit something after all this, and it might as well be someone who deserves it."

"We're here," I said in place of an answer.

"Yeah? That doesn't mean you and I are done." He looked out his window to Rhea's little project home and immediately noted the landscaping. "Textbook Rhea," he said and got out of the car the moment I put it in park.

Seeing Ben in Rhea's front yard brought the reality of the situation down on me. Ben and Rhea were about to see each other in the very place she'd come to hide from him. And Ty? The guy was going to flip. At least he'd better, or Rhea would be one step closer to believing that walking away was a good choice. All I could hope was that Ty had the guts to face off with Ben in a way that would convince Rhea that he was in their relationship all the way. He'd said the words, but she needed something more.

Worst of all, they needed to do it all without an audience. Besides, I needed to get some shopping done. Once Ben was done talking to Rhea, I did not want him in public. I needed to get him back to my place and try to get him to stay there so he wouldn't go out and start a fight somewhere.

But before I got moving, I needed to make sure everyone connected. I took a deep breath and got out of the car as well. Two driveways over, Ty's truck was parked at his place. He was home, which made it likely he was with Rhea, unless he was letting her wedge them further apart.

To my surprise, Ben didn't head straight for the door, but moved through the front yard touching plants I didn't know the names of.

"It's amazing the stuff you miss," he mused, as if not caring if I heard or not. "I pass by her old house sometimes and Emily has petunias planted there now. Petunias! Rhea would go into shiver shock if she saw. But this?" His smile was the saddest I'd ever seen it. "I could have picked this house as hers out of a thousand."

I didn't have time to answer before the door swung open, and Rhea took three quick steps to edge of her porch.

"Ben?" she whispered.

He straightened, looking as yummy as a dripping ice cream cone. "Hey."

I was ready for anything from Rhea. She'd been such a spaz lately that the reaction menu was wide open. What did happen, though, happened so fast that I'm not sure if she ran or simply leaped off the porch in to Ben's arms. Whichever it was, he caught her as easily as a pillow.

"I've missed you," he said, holding her tight as both her arms and legs wrapped around him as if she couldn't imagine letting go. Ever.

Where was Ty? This would be his cue to freak out.

After several seconds, Rhea's eyes found mine over Ben's

shoulder. It was a relief to see gratitude in her eyes. Happy day. She wasn't going to go through a phase of hating me before realizing why I'd done this.

"Did you just get in?" she asked him.

"Just." Ben's arms tightened around her, but his voice was light. "Kate says you've got big drama going on and that if I came out here, I'd get to say 'I told you so.' "

Rhea flinched at that, but only I saw it. As if realizing the picture they made, Rhea unwound her limbs from Ben's body and slid down. He reluctantly let her go.

"Is there a decent place to eat around here?" he complained, although I saw him catch her change in mood. "I need protein."

She nodded, heading back to her front door. "Absolutely. Let me get my keys." Saying nothing else, she ran up the steps, and Ben whirled on me.

"What the hell is going on?" he whispered.

I shrugged as if to say, I told you so.

"Not one joke?" he pressed, pointing down to his belt buckle. "She didn't even make fun of my belt. She hates this belt." I knew that. Everyone who ever knew Rhea and Ben in college knew how much she hated that belt buckle. "I don't even think she saw it before tackling me."

There was no reason for me to respond.

"Is it the guy?" he pressed, looking violent. "Is it Ty that's got her all wound up?"

I shook my head. "Get her to tell you, and you'll understand."

Ben did not look convinced. "Where is this preppy boy anyway?" he sneered, and as if on cue Ty walked out his front door two doors down with his phone pressed to his ear. Rhea had called him. Good girl.

Taking one look at the competition, Ty said something into the phone and made quick work of the short distance between their houses. Ben followed my eyes and gave Ty a look over as Rhea moved out the front door. She didn't call out to either guy, but her eyes darted between the two as if expecting fists to fly. This was Ben, after all, and the guy was hotheaded on the best of days.

"He's short," Ben muttered, even though Ty and I were about the same height without shoes. Ty's eyes singled me out of the group and burned into me as he drew close. He knew I was behind Ben's presence in Salt Lake, and he wasn't happy about it. But once he crossed onto Rhea's property line, his focus was on Ben. And Ben was looking right back.

"You Ty?" he asked, his hand fisting at his side.

"Yeah, that's—"

Ben's punch shot out with such blinding speed that I actually squealed and stepped back. Ty, however, seemed completely prepared for it, as one muscular arm parried the punch away and the other slammed into Ben's jaw with a force that had him rocking on his heels.

"Ty!" Rhea cried out, racing forward to get between the two. "He's just here to talk."

Clearly ready to go around, Ty kept eye contact with Ben over Rhea's shoulder. "Really? It didn't look like that to me."

Rhea stepped away, her face borderlining on cold. "I called to tell you I was going to take Ben out, not to ask your permission, Ty." She turned and faced Ben, who was trying hard not to touch his jaw. "Get in the car, Ben. I'll be right there."

The smug look Ben shot Ty before doing as he was asked was as incendiary as any punch. And Rhea had to put her hand on Ty's chest to remind them that this was her turf and these were her rules.

"We're just going to talk, Ty. Do I get jealous when your sister comes to town?"

Ty stabbed a finger at Ben. "That is not your brother!"

"Well, he's as close as I've got, and I need him right now,

okay?" She didn't mean for them to, but I saw her words hit him like a punch in the gut. And once she saw them land, she didn't take them back. "We're just going to go talk in a public place, Ty. That's it. And if you don't trust me to do that, then we're done."

Rhea didn't wait for an answer. She didn't even offer an encouraging smile. She just walked away, leaving a confused and hurt Ty behind. Totally harsh. Even I wasn't that bad . . . okay, maybe I was, but it was hard to watch.

"Let her go," I said, moving in and touching his arm. Only then did I realize that the guy actually had tears in his eyes. Tears he quickly blinked away.

"What's going on here, Kathryn?" he asked, his voice cracking slightly.

"The inevitable," I answered, wishing I had more time to spend with him. "Ben's known Rhea her whole life. He knows Elliott. He knows everything except for how she's changed in the past five months, and she needs him. Not only with the Elliott situation, but with you. He's not the enemy here, Ty. He's here to make sure you're right for her."

"If you say so," he muttered, obviously having picked up on the chemistry Rhea and Ben had never really lost.

"But at least you did one thing right," I said, backing to my car. "You didn't let him hit you."

Ty tensed at the memory. "Does he always do that?"

I shook my head. "Only when he wants to feel someone out. And because you passed that test, let me give you a hint. When Rhea comes back, don't be sensible. She'll try to be, but after talking to Ben for a couple hours, she won't need more talking. Kiss her, Ty. If you want to keep her, you will kiss the living daylights out of her until she can't remember what she wanted to say." I walked around to the driver's side of my car and opened the door. "But if you decide breaking up might be the right choice before she comes back, then sit down and have that rational discussion. She'll let you go, and she'll make it easy for you. It's your choice."

I got into the car out of self-defense, mostly. I didn't want to hear what Ty had to say. I didn't want him to ask me if I thought they should break up. I didn't want to interfere any more than I already had. It was all up to Rhea, Ben, and Ty now. And by the end of the day, things were definitely going to be different. I'd brought Ben to Utah and left Ty questioning whether he really wanted a place in Rhea's complicated life. The rest was up to him, and I needed to make sure Ty was the only guy Ben tried to start a fight with that day.

NINETEEN

I WAS ONLY HOME *for three days, but something had happened in my absence. Something big, and no one was talking about it.*

Isaac, Aaron, Danny, and Ben only shrugged when I asked about it. I'd missed a concert and quite a few classes by their count but nothing more. Yet no one from the fraternities or sororities would look at me—and not because they were snubbing me. They looked afraid.

And since no one felt like answering my questions, I did what any aspiring reporter would do. I checked the paper.

While I was gone, the frat house where I had been drugged and raped—yes, I could say the word now—had burned down. The fire had started in the wine cellar by one of the many torches used for light. Arson was being investigated, since that same week the fraternity had lost school sponsorship due to a horrific hazing stunt interrupted by the astronomy club. The reporter left the gratuitousness of the haze to reader's imagination and merely highlighted the fact that four of the boys had withdrawn from the university after being discovered, while the other eight were undergoing mandatory counseling. Some believed that the fraternity burned the house down to protest being evicted.

Somehow I doubted that. Yet I was left with the same question I'd started with: What happened while I was gone? And how

*much of a role, if any, had my new friends played in all of it?
And did I really care?*

* * *

Do you have drinks at your place, or do I need to hit a bar?

Ben's text, while expected, landed in my phone's inbox a
bit ahead of schedule. Luckily, he had a key to my place, and I
had a trunk stocked full of what he liked.

Open bar at my place, I typed back. *Beer in the fridge and
I'm bring the real stuff now.*

The guy was hurting, which was fine. Maybe it was time,
really. Rhea had been his ace in the hole for how long? He'd
never stepped up. He had to have known that someone else
would and that Rhea deserved nothing less.

I loved Ben with everything I had. As a friend, there was
no one better. As a boyfriend, he sucked eggs. Rhea had tried
to straddle an impossible line between those two truths for far
too long. So long that she couldn't look devotion in the eye and
believe it was real when she looked at Ty. I had my own issues
to deal with when it came to men, but Rhea wasn't without her
own baggage. Her whole life she'd loved a man who had no
internal sense of fidelity. Ben was always quick to find a new
girl, which was why Rhea thought breaking up with Ty would
only hurt her.

Taking a deep breath as I put my key in the lock, I prayed
that somewhere nearby Ty was following my advice as I opened
the door and smelled cologne and leather mixed with my usual
air freshener. Ben was already reclined on the couch, drinking.
"Well, I never thought I'd say this, but our Rhea is in love."

"Yeah," I agreed, bringing my bag of bottles over to the bar
and unloading it. No drinking for me tonight. I knew too well
how dumb Ben got when he drank, and the last thing I needed
to do was open myself to his charisma. If I drank, I would flirt.
If I flirted, he would proposition me. Again.

That was the number one reason I would never approve of Rhea and Ben as a couple. When Rhea hurt Ben, Ben got drunk and tried to hook up with me for payback. I'd never told Rhea this and clearly, neither had Ben. I didn't see a reason to unless the two of them made moves to get back together. If that happened, I'd air all the dirty laundry, but until then, I could deal with a wannabe rock star who drank so he could talk himself into doing regrettable things. On that level, I was the last one who could throw stones.

"He's not at all what I pictured her falling for," Ben said, staring at my wall while I poured some cranberry juice. I needed to look like I was drinking. "Her dad's so quiet. I always thought she'd go for someone like that."

I shook my head and took a seat next to him. "No way. Rhea doesn't need quiet. She needs to be reminded that life is more than just a task list of to-do items."

Ben's nose scrunched. "But this guy? He's like everything we mocked growing up. A pretty boy jock who's used to having girls fall at his feet? Rhea hates those guys."

He had a point. "You don't know Ty. He's a bit different."

"So I hear," he snorted, then brought his fingers up to his jaw. "At least he can punch, but I think Rhea taught him how. He left behind her signature sting."

"They train together," I confirmed.

Ben looked at me then, his eyes somber. "Is he going to cheat on her?"

I laughed out loud, throwing my head back to let the mocking sound flow more easily. This question from him? "Like you? No. Not a chance."

"I never cheated on her," Ben objected.

"Oh, please! How many women did you dangle in front of her face, trying to get her to beg for you back?"

"That's not cheating," he pressed, not denying that he'd done it.

"You knew she was in love with you, and purposefully hurt her, Ben. You spent nearly every waking moment being her best friend and confidant and then forced her to watch as you picked up the next pretty young thing. What do you want to call that if not cheating?"

"Women!" he groaned. "You make everything out like men are always the bad guys. Rhea was there too, you know. She could have stepped up and told the other girls to get lost. I gave her every opportunity."

It was no use talking to him about the past. If he couldn't see the role he played in losing Rhea, there was no way I could help him.

"Whatever," I said. "The point is that Ty's perfect for Rhea. And if they get past all the crap pulling them apart now, they're going to be an unstoppable couple. He's awesome, Ben."

He scowled when I said that, as if he wanted me to take it back. "This coming from the woman whose preferred use for men is as a stepping stone?"

There was a light smack in his accusation, but I had to own it. "Yes."

"Hmm. I hate him more now." He downed the remaining liquid in his glass and took a deep breath. "She wants to marry him, you know."

"I know."

He processed that. "If the preppy boy wants her, he can't let her think about it too hard. No long engagement."

"Agreed."

"It's just a few weeks to Thanksgiving, and after that there's no good date until spring, and she has to be married by St. Patrick's Day, according to the deal with the crime boss guy, right?"

"Yeah," I said, liking that he was carrying on the conversation for both of us.

He shook his head. "They're either getting married in the

next three weeks or not at all. She'll want it at her dad's place, and it will be too cold in a bit."

Sometimes Ben could think like a girl. Swearing under his breath, he turned and looked at me.

"Three weeks?" he repeated and then swore again. "Man, I need another drink."

"It won't change anything."

He tipped his glass at me and cocked an eyebrow. "Never say never," he said and stood to go check out the spread I'd delivered. I could never tell how much Ben had in system by his walk. Like me, he carried liquor well everywhere but his head. He was looking to do something stupid tonight.

"I'm not letting you go back over there tonight if you're drunk," I said.

"Fair enough," he agreed. "Besides, I already promised Rhea I wouldn't go over unless she called."

And the only reason she would call was if she and Ty had a messy break up. "Well, let's hope that doesn't happen."

He grunted, not exactly in agreement. "Any place to play pool around here or something? Or local bands? Anything worth hearing? Word on the street is that Neon Trees started up in Provo, and they don't suck. How far away is that?"

I laughed. I couldn't help it. "Trust me, Ben. You do not want to go to Provo. Ever." Or if he did, I didn't want to go with him. The night would end with someone getting arrested. Probably Ben.

"Well, something else then. Who else is from here? Royal Bliss? There's got to be something decent going on in the underground tonight."

Unfortunately, Rhea was the one who would be dialed in there, and I wasn't bothering her right then. No way.

"It's the weekend," I said. "We can just wander. All the bars are quarantined to certain areas anyway, so we're bound to find something. Let me just change into something more appropriate."

"Nice," he said, going half and half with Crown and Coke. I'd have to watch that boy once we hit the street. As docile as he was acting now, he had fight in him. "Need some help changing?"

And so it began. "Not even a little," I said, disappearing into my room. "And if you come in, you're going to get a stiletto in the eye—and you know I won't miss."

"Yes'm," he called out from the other side of the door while I opened my closet and eyed my evening attire. I'd dressed for an evening out far too infrequently since moving to Utah, and for a moment I couldn't choose what I wanted to wear the most. My cute little Fendi number was probably just a little too sexy for the occasion. I needed something hot that didn't look like I was trying too hard, and to switch my make-up from a day to night look.

My coffee-colored Halston dress with a bulky Gucci necklace would be quick, hot, and understated. As nice as my Miu Mius would look with that, I wasn't in the mood for serious heels. Plus I was in Utah. A boot was best to cover some leg. The make-up would take me five minutes, and I'd be out the door on the arm of a guy who would turn heads just by existing. It wasn't fair, really, but complaining was useless.

Six minutes later, I moved back out to the living room prepared for the wolf whistle I got.

"You look like a million bucks there, Kate."

I shot him a warning. "It's been a while since I've gone out on a Saturday, so don't think I'm dressing up for you."

He put his glass down. "A guy can think what he wants."

"Says the guy currently in a serious relationship," I reminded him, holding up my keys. "Let's get out of here. You get to carry these."

"We driving?"

"Nope. This town is small. Everything's close." I led him to the front door, we walked out into the hall, and I locked the door behind us.

"Good. That means I might just get a chance to defend your honor tonight."

I gave a short laugh but didn't comment. Honor wasn't something I was exactly overflowing with, it seemed. But sure, Ben could defend whatever little bit still remained. As long as it didn't become a news story.

"So where are we starting out?" he asked. "Have a favorite bar yet?"

My lips pursed in amusement as I called the elevator. "Are you kidding? I've been here a month and spent the whole time with Rhea or at work. How many bars do you think I've been to?"

"Good point," he agreed, shooting me a conspiratorial look just as the elevator doors started to open. "Well, then, it's good that I'm here to show you a good time."

It was impossible not to flirt a little back. "Good thing," I agreed, stepping into the elevator and sending a courtesy smile to its lone occupant. The second I made eye contact with him, all oxygen in the immediate vicinity seemed to disappear. I must have stumbled slightly when Dahl and I locked gazes, because I felt Ben catch some of my weight as he sent a curious look to Dahl. Ben wasn't stupid. He knew something was up.

"Going down?" Ben asked, hitting the lobby button.

Clearly Dahl wasn't, since none of the other elevator buttons were currently glowing. He'd been coming to my floor for some reason only he knew. So far he sucked at avoiding me.

After about five seconds, Ben sent me a look, and I knew he had figured out who Dahl was, even though I'd never even referenced him. Not good. Ben probably had about six shots in him, which was enough for him to get lippy. Worse yet, Dahl might be able to smell it on him.

Not talking was the best option.

"Know any good local bands?" Ben asked, his tone innocuous even as he placed a possessive arm around me. Dahl noticed, which stupidly had my heart giving a few excited pumps even as I noted how the cotton of his shirt stretched across his chest.

"Can't say I do," Dahl bit out.

Silence. Only a few floors to go. It took only a glance at Dahl to get a clue as to what he was thinking—what anyone in his position would be thinking. He thought Ben and I were on a date. That I'd had my fun with the lawyer and had moved on to a bad boy. Well, it was probably best he kept thinking that. Made things simpler.

At long last, the elevators doors opened, and Ben led me out, leaving Dahl to follow. I would have preferred it the other way around, but it was an awkward point to force, so I went with the flow as Ben led me across the lobby to the exit. Behind us, I could have sworn that I felt Dahl fuming as if I'd done something wrong, and by the set of Ben's jaw, I saw that he and Dahl hadn't started out on the right foot. I needed to tell Ben he was dealing with a cop so he would know that this was not the fight he was looking for that night.

But how?

Like any gentleman would, Ben moved a step ahead to open the door for me. Once I passed through he kept holding it for Dahl.

"Have a good one," Ben said.

"Yeah," Dahl agreed. "Looks like one of us will."

The words were so unexpected from Dahl's mouth that I was still trying to figure out if I had actually heard them when the sick *thunk* of flesh impacting bone rang out and Dahl's right knee buckled. Before he could fall or even register what had happened, though, Ben had caught him by the collar, hauled him up, and clocked him again. This time, Dahl was expecting the punch and merely staggered back, covering his face. Not missing a beat, Ben went for his ribs.

"What did you just say?" he yelled at Dahl.

"Ben, stop!" I cried out, looking around to see if there

were any witnesses, but the street was empty.

Rather than stop, he pushed Dahl to the ground. "You have no idea what you're talking about!" he snarled. "Apologize now!"

Both furious and bloodied, Dahl looked between us at a complete loss for words as Ben got right back into his face.

"How long have you even known this woman?" he pressed, stabbing a finger my direction. "A few weeks, maybe? A whole month? Well, I've known her for eight years, and she is one of my best friends, so you'd better know exactly what you're talking about before you start throwing words like that around."

That last verbal parting blow hit Dahl harder than any of the punches. I could see it in his eyes, and I had to admit, it felt really good for Ben to put him in his place. Even if I didn't exactly deserve it.

Ben moved toward Dahl again. I didn't know what he was thinking, but knew it couldn't be a good idea. He'd made his point rather perfectly in my opinion.

A touch of my hand stopped his forward motion. "Ben, no. He's a cop."

To my surprise, Ben smiled at this news and sent Dahl a winning smile. "Well, I hope you press charges then. I'd love to go and tell all your coworkers why your face looks like hamburger." He moved over and took my hand. "I assume you have Kate's number. Give her a call if you decide you want to have me arrested. We'll be somewhere with a pool table or a live band. Or both."

We started away, with Ben practically dragging me behind him as I tried to process what just happened. After a quick look at Dahl, I decided that he probably wasn't going to charge Ben for assault. And as for my knight in shining armor, you would never think he just pounded another man into the ground. He looked relaxed and loose and even sent me a bemused look.

"So, any truth to what he said back there? You been getting around?"

That was Ben for you. Punch first and ask questions later. "Maybe a bit."

His eyebrows shot up. "You've been here, what, four weeks and haven't even had time to hit a bar, but you've been able to get that reputation? Sounds like you owe me a few stories."

"I guess," I agreed and started talking.

TWENTY

WHAT ABOUT THIS one?" I asked, holding up a black knit top. Half my wardrobe consisted of black now since that was all I could wear to work.

Rhea's eyes barely glanced at my find. "It's dated. You could probably find it at a discount store for more than half off. Big spenders will know that."

I worked for commission, and Rhea was very aware of that. Fashion didn't come naturally to me, but with Rhea as a mentor I was catching on. "How do you know that?"

She walked up and rubbed the fabric between her hands. "Feel it. Cotton and rayon. Spring line and economical. Is that how you want to be perceived by your customers? Dated and low maintenance?"

"Um, no?" I was assuming that wasn't a trick question.

She nodded. "Your customers want to stand out in a good way, which means you need to do the same." She walked over to a display of tops similar to the one I'd picked up and brought it back to hold up against mine. "See the difference?"

Besides the fact that the one she had chosen was way cuter and twice the price, I knew that wasn't what she was asking. "My fabric is shinier?"

"Feel it."

*I did as commanded, surprised to find it both light and soft.
"I like it."*

*"Bamboo," she said simply. "You'll notice the difference now,
just like your customers already do."*

"Is bamboo better?" I asked, trying not to gasp at the price tag.

*She shrugged. "It falls under eco-fashion. Bamboo is a renew-
able resource. People who are environmentally aware care more
than people who aren't. Customers like that will notice and probably want to support you over another sales rep who doesn't care as
much about the environment."*

*Easy to say for the girl with a bottomless bank account. I had
a monthly allowance now, though. That and my phone back. My
daddy had put his foot down on that when I insisted on coming
back to college. In exchange, I had to promise not to take any more
money from Rhea, since Mama imagined her family to be Muslim
extremists. No matter how many times I said it, she wouldn't
believe her dad was a white man from Texas who married an
immigrant.*

*"You don't have to get that one," she said, probably notic-
ing that I was doing math in my head to see if I could afford it.
"There's a lot more where that came from. I was just making a
point. Clothes should be tactical. Don't just buy something to buy
something. Buy it because you know what it will do for you."*

*As many times as I'd heard words like that spoken to me over
the years, it was like I heard them for the first time. I mean, dress
for success? How cliché is that? Everyone had heard that. But,
"Clothes should be tactical"? Those simple words planted a seed in
me that opened my eyes in a whole new way as I replaced the shirt
to its display and reassessed my surroundings.*

* * *

Ben took the first flight out in the morning. I'm pretty sure
he didn't sleep, even though I did. The TV in my living room
stayed on all night, and when I got up, the bottle of Crown

Royal I'd bought for him was empty. The man could still walk any line a cop threw at him though. It was actually impressive.

"I'll tell Rhea's dad to prep the gardens," he said as I pulled up to the curbside drop off.

He seemed deflated, lost. "Ben, are you okay?"

He shook his head. "Nope. But I've got a kid to get home to. Tell Rhea I say bye."

"Or you could call her," I suggested. "We both know she's awake."

"No. She'll know and she'll come. It wouldn't be fair to do that to her."

He wasn't making sense. "She'll know what?"

"Nothing," he mumbled. "Nothing. I need to get home." He cracked open the door. "I'm glad I got to punch that loser for you last night, though. Promise to stay away from him?"

"I don't even have to try," I said. "In a few weeks, our paths won't cross at all."

"Unless he stalks you at your condo. Cop or not, you should be able to ban him."

I chewed my lip. "We'll see."

Ben grabbed my hand and dropped a kiss on it. "Love you, Kate, but I have to get out of here. Call me, though. And Isaac misses you. Call him too."

"Absolutely," I agreed, feeling myself choke up. "I miss you. A lot. Know that. I'll visit as soon as I can."

"Maybe for the wedding," he said with mock cheerfulness. "We'll see."

He gripped his small carry-on, staring into space for a moment. "Life really doesn't turn out how you plan, does it?"

"Nope," I said, then we both laughed. I squeezed his hand. "I love you, Ben. Thanks for being you—even if you are an absolute screw-up."

"Right back at you," he said, stepping out of the car. That was it. He just walked off, shoulders drooping slightly. No wave or backwards glance. He looked like a tired rock star who'd been touring too long.

In Ben's mind, Rhea had made the decision last night. She'd chosen Ty, but I wasn't that easily convinced. She'd let Ben go, yes. But that didn't mean she would pull a repeat act on Ty. I needed to talk to her ASAP.

Pulling into traffic to exit the airport, I called her. I knew she'd answer.

"Morning." Her voice was cautious.

"Ben says bye," I said, letting her know he was gone.

Rhea took a deep breath. "How was he?"

"Shaken and resigned." She deserved to know the truth. "But he'll be fine."

"Yeah," she agreed. "He will be."

"I was just thinking that we missed riding on Friday, and you don't have church for over six hours. Want me to swing by and pick you up?"

"That would actually be perfect," she said, relief heavy in her voice for some reason I didn't know yet.

"I'm already dressed, so I can be there in about fifteen."

"I'll be waiting," she said, and we hung up.

TWENTY-ONE

MY NEWFOUND SNOBBERY had me raising an eyebrow when Rhea stopped us in front of a Pac Sun at the mall.

"What are we doing here?" I asked, itching to get home with my prize purchases.

Rhea stared at the store like a death sentence. "Waiting for me to swallow my pride."

I glanced to the store and back at her. "Why?"

She looked at me, her eyes resigned. "Because clothes should be tactical."

"Uh, is that supposed to make sense?"

She shifted back and forth, sliding her hands into her back pockets. "I told you I've been training with that Elliott guy, right?"

I nodded. "You mentioned it."

"Well, he told me if I could get a certain job done for him, he would do me a favor. And I want that favor."

Elliott had access to something Rhea actually wanted and couldn't get for herself? I couldn't imagine such a thing. "And it requires you to go into Pac Sun?"

Her head bobbed. "I need to fit in the environment he's sending me into. Trendy and underestimated."

"Oh." What could I say to that? "Well, it's best just to jump in then. Just like cold water. Don't torture yourself."

"Yeah," she agreed. "You're right." But she didn't move.

I pointed to a clearance rack labeled: EVERYTHING $10 OR LESS. "We can start there. If there's one thing Mama taught me, it's how to bargain shop, so I'm 'it' this time. Tag me and I'll show you how it's done."

At last her frosty eyes melted a bit, and I caught a trace of a smile. "Tag you?"

"You know, like the game you played when you were a kid."

For some reason she thought that was funny as her hand flipped out and gave my arm a light smack. "Fine, then. Tag. You're it."

"Was that so hard? Now let's get you dressed for success," I said and pulled her forward by her elbow.

* * *

After initial sprints, our horses settled into a lazy pace that allowed Rhea and I to talk.

"Ben punched Dahl?" Rhea asked in surprise after I told her the story. "I mean, not that I'm surprised that Ben hit him—more that Dahl deserved it."

"Seriously." In fact, I still played those moments over and over in my head trying to excuse Dahl somehow, but no. For a few rare moments of his life he'd been completely out of line.

"You've had a heavy few days," she said.

"You've had a heavy few weeks," I shot back. "I'm sorry I was so distracted that it took a while for me to catch on."

"I didn't want you to," she replied. "There's no easy answer for me right now, Kay. I don't even know if there's a right answer."

"Still?" I asked, wondering how things went yesterday. "What did Ben have to say about it all?"

She shook her head, her expression half way between amused and worried. "He wants to shoot Elliott in his sleep and scatter his body parts so he can never be laid to rest."

"Nice," I said, laughing only because I knew it wouldn't

happen. "What did he say about Ty?"

"He wanted to know what I could possibly see in him. He calls him a preppy runt."

"Ty is Rhea-sized," I decided. "You can wear four-inch heels, and he's still a hair taller. That's all you need. In regular shoes, you just have to tilt up, he tilts down, and you're ready to kiss."

A Mona Lisa smile crept across her face. "Yeah."

"Oh, now you have to tell me. How did last night go?"

She sent me a sideways look. "He followed your advice."

A surge of hope pulsed through me. "Which part of it?"

"The first part, I believe. The one that included not talking."

I threw my head back and laughed, calling out into the morning sky, "That man is so smart!"

"Yeah, it was—" She paused, searched for the right words. "It was eye opening."

"Also known as awesome?"

Another quiet smile lit her face. "Amazing. And you were right. When I left Ben, I thought breaking up with Ty was the right thing. I don't have a life he needs to walk into. It's too much to ask of anyone. The chances of him dying if he stays with me are significant. All Donald Smith and his little gang have to do to get me to do anything is threaten Ty. That puts me in a very bad position and Ty in an even worse one."

"But that's his choice," I inserted.

"A choice he doesn't understand." Her voice sounded tired. "But we've already talked in that circle."

"I think Ty's stronger than you want to believe he is. And I think he understands your position and wants to make sure you don't have to face everything alone."

A shocking thing happened when those words left my mouth. Rhea cried. Not a gentle trickle that sneaked down her cheek with dignity, but a sudden sob that had her leaning forward and resting on Hermes's neck. The rush of tears didn't last too long, but she was leaning on Hermes when she said, "My mind plays tricks on me when I think of being with him. I see everything being fine. I'm not alone. Next March just disappears in some little happy fantasy where everything just turns out fine."

"You're both going to make it through March, Rhea. So is Ty. You know that don't you?"

She sat up, shaking her head. "There's no way to know that."

"No?" I asked, feeling a little offended. "Well, let's look at all the people The Fours would have to kill to get away with killing you. Not only would Ty have to go, but a big-mouthed reporter and every member of a rising rock band that just got signed with Mercury Records." I watched while that realization sank in and went on. "They'd have to kill your millionaire father and your uncle and aunt, just to start with. These are influential people, Rhea. People who don't disappear easily and who are fiercely loyal to you. When March seventeenth comes around, the biggest mistake Donald Smith can make is to underestimate you and your support system. We're not going to let you die. Ty either."

She took a deep, shaky breath. "Wow. I hadn't thought of that."

"Well, think about it really hard. Because it's a fact."

We rode along in silence while she processed that. "I've spent a lot of time recently thinking about how much has changed since I moved to Utah. It's like everything unraveled for me the day I met those missionaries. I lost Ben. I left my job, family, and friends and just ran away. It just seems like ever since I got baptized, my life has been a mess."

Her words were music to my ears, and it actually hurt that I needed to contradict her. "Becoming a Mormon isn't the worst thing you've done."

Rhea's sidelong look of surprise at those words leaving my mouth was worthy of a Kodak moment.

"I know, I know," I conceded. "I never thought I'd say it either, but just look at how much your life has changed in the past few months."

"Uh, yeah. Everything's fallen apart."

Again, it killed me to correct her, but I had to. "The problems that have surfaced weren't brought about by you being Mormon, Rhea. They were already there, mostly thanks to Elliott." I was right and she knew it.

"As heartwarming as it is to think about how all of you would rally to save me, the truth is that whatever happens in March is not something I want to drag you into. I definitely don't want you to follow in my footsteps. Whatever it is, I'm doing it alone." She sent me one of her steady, unflinching looks. "That's just a fact, so get used to it now."

"Maybe," I conceded. "You won't know that until you know what he wants."

She looked off into the horizon. "Or I could just leave now and go back to L.A. If I work with Elliott again, everything else will be off the table because I'll be in his jurisdiction."

"Uh-huh." We both knew that option would be soul killing. "And what would your new religion think about you voluntarily working for a—what do they call them?"

"Secret combination," she said.

"Yeah. One of those."

"They'll excommunicate me, for sure."

"So," I mused sarcastically. "If you go back to L.A., you lose your religion, the man of your dreams, and essentially your soul. Sounds like a great deal."

"But Ty would be safe," she qualified.

"Oh, come down off that cross already," I groaned. "Rhea, as your friend, it's my job to tell you when you're not thinking straight. And you're not. Not even a little. You're delusional if you think you can go back to Elliott knowing what you know now. At some point, you're going to stand up to both him and Donald. Might as well do it in March with an awesome husband whose very existence proves that you are not who they want you to be."

"Well, tell me what you really think," she chuckled.

"I'm serious! They don't think you're capable of marriage. They have you profiled as some lone wolf that they want to turn into an assassin at best. If you convince yourself that it's your job to save Ty by walking away from him, I swear you're going to prove them right, Rhea. They'll get you to kill someone—no matter how hard you try to avoid it. And once you do that, there's no going back. You know it. They'll have you."

Again, she didn't respond immediately. "You've thought this through a bit."

"You bet I have. They'll kill me just as soon as killing Ty, but if you walked away from me in order to save me, I might just kill you myself." She chuckled even though I was being serious. "The truth is that none of us know how this is going to shake out. All we have is today. All we have is now."

"Sufficient to the day is the evil thereof," she muttered and I remembered reading that somewhere.

"Yeah, that. Maybe we should look into a happier way to say it, but yes. Don't let what you're fearing in five months shape what you do today. When you show up, The Fours may just want you to do something simple. You don't know, so stop empowering them."

Rhea closed her eyes, and I wondered for a moment if she was praying or something, when she started confessing. "Part of me panics at the thought of leaving the business. It's all I really know. But at the same time, I feel this weird peace—like all this is preparing me for something else. That same voice is the one that tells me to follow my heart, not my mind on this one."

The moment she said the words, I realized I was tuning into the same "voice." Like I'd told Dahl, if it weren't for Rhea, I wouldn't believe in God. Normally I laugh when people talk about God's "plan" for them. More often than not, they cited those plans as an excuse to give up because God had another path for them somewhere. But when Rhea said the words, I could suddenly see how God might make a plan for someone like her. After all, what couldn't God do with a woman who was rich, influential, fearless, beautiful, disciplined, and talented?

The options were bordering on endless.

"It sounds stupid when I say that out loud," Rhea back-pedaled.

"No, I get it," I said, and suddenly I felt a conviction I hadn't felt in a long time. Rhea was going to survive this. By some miracle, she was going to squeak through and get a really sweet happily ever after. "You've got to take the scary path here and break ties with these guys, Rhea. You've got to put it all on the line and fight for it."

She turned, giving me a searching look that allowed me a rare peek into her soul. She was scared.

"Even if it kills me?" she asked.

The question wasn't rhetorical, and her eyes held mine as she waited for an answer.

"Even if it kills you," I agreed. It wouldn't. I knew it. And deep down, Rhea did too, but she needed to face the worst possible scenario and accept it before she could feel peace.

"Let Ty love you, Rhea. Just like you let me love you in my own way. And Ben, and everyone else. Imagine, if you will, that you mean more to us than we do to you. Part of me would die if you walked away from me. Part of Ty would die, too. You're the only one who can really kill him, not The Fours." I sounded so profound. It was kind of surreal. "So break up with him if you want to, but do it for the right reasons."

"Wow," she breathed. "And to think I came out here in

case I had any good advice for you."

I laughed. "Surprise! For once I'm not thinking about myself."

"I didn't mean that. You've just had a rough few days, and we never talked about how things were going with you and Dahl in the mountains. I mean, you were actually kissing him."

"Yeah," I agreed. "He may not want to do it again, but at least he taught me why I've always had problems in that area. I can thank him for that."

She nodded, clearly wanting to say something but choosing not to.

"What?" I prompted.

Her eyes wouldn't meet mine at first, but then she looked over. "Don't do that to me again, okay?"

She didn't want to say what, and she didn't have to. I knew.

"Kay, I'm not judging you here. You know I'm not, but I don't think you know how it felt to watch you and Alan on Friday. I can't do that again."

"Yeah, I think I may have finally learned my lesson there. He was pretty bad." I paused for a second, noting Rhea's hopeful look. "I mean, you know I'm scraping bottom when I sleep with someone who can't even boost my career."

She didn't want to laugh but did even as she said, "Not funny."

I laughed right along with her. "It's funny because it's true." I sent her a look that let her know things were going to change. "It tweaks with your mind when you know that a couple of dozen men have had their way with you, and you have no idea who they are, except for one or two." I'd never confessed that before, not even to a therapist when confronted with the question. "Every time some guy opened the door for me or I caught someone smiling at me, I wondered. I didn't want to—I tried not to, but the desire was there to prove that I could use and reject them too."

Rhea said nothing, just listened, her eyes so soulful that I wondered just how much watching me over the years had affected her.

"I felt safe with Ben and Isaac, but that made sense. And when I met Ty, he felt safe too. He was so in love with you that he never looked at me in a way that made me want to prove to him that he was dirt."

"I noticed," she said. "The first time I saw you two together on my front porch, I noticed how relaxed you were. You let him give you a tour while I wasn't even there. You even smiled about it."

It surprised me she would remember such a specific detail. "Good memory."

She smiled. "I try to pay attention."

If that wasn't the understatement of the year, I didn't know what was. "Tell you what," I mused. "If you decide to break up with Ty, I'll marry him."

A leather riding glove smacked into the side of my head and I caught it before it fell into the dirt.

"Not funny!" Rhea said.

"No?" I threw the glove back at her. "Then marry the man and put us all out of our misery."

"I get it, okay? You approve."

"I approve and I covet," I teased. "One day our roles are going to be reversed, Rhea, and you'll see how frustrating it is to see someone walk away from perfection."

"Note taken. Can we move on to something else?"

"Lunch?" I offered. "I've got a whole bunch of food Ben didn't touch. Want to help me with it?"

"Sounds good," she agreed as we turned our mounts back toward the stables.

TWENTY-TWO

I SHOULD HAVE BEEN *studying, but instead I was driving to the beach based on Ben's hunch that something was wrong with Rhea. She hadn't shown up for band practice.*

Clearly, the sky must have fallen. The guy was all drama when it came to Rhea.

It was odd that she was at the beach alone, though. She went everywhere with her crew. But she'd been different ever since that private security guy had taken her under his wing. She always seemed to be off somewhere, doing something she didn't want to talk about. And it didn't take a genius to see why that would rub Ben wrong.

Parking my car in the lot, I followed Rhea's instructions until I saw her sitting just where her text said she would be. She wasn't wearing a swim suit, which was my first cue that Ben's concerns hadn't been off the mark. She just sat with her back to the world and her face to the incoming tide.

I took off my shoes and padded over to her. "This seat taken?" I asked and sat without waiting for a reply. A smart move on my part, because a response wasn't necessarily forthcoming. Something was definitely wrong, and I only had one guess.

"Did Elliott find your aunt for you?"

Rather than replying, she leaned to one side to grab a folder she'd sat on to keep it from blowing away in the wind. Once in hand, she brushed the sand off and held it out to me, never making eye contact. It felt wrong to take the folder, but I did, opening it with reverence. My somberness was sabotaged by the fact that I had no idea what I was looking at. A certificate? Whatever it was, it wasn't in English.

"A death certificate," Rhea said, sensing my confusion.

That wasn't good. "Who died?"

"My aunt," she said, her eyes locked on the horizon, bereft of any expression. "I'm the only living female in my mom's line, it seems."

My first instinct was to think she was exaggerating to make a point, but Rhea wasn't that type. She was being literal, and for some reason being the only living female in her mother's line was very important to her.

Afraid to say the wrong thing, I flipped to the next page, which was in English, so I knew it was an autopsy. Half of the words were foreign to me, but cause and date of death were easy enough to discern. Cause of death was listed as a stroke, and quick math showed that Rhea's mom had been thirty-four when she died.

That was so young! A stroke at thirty-four? And Rhea's aunt was dead too? How old had she been?

I looked back to the first certificate, recognizing only numbers, but it was enough to draw a picture that might be the reason for Rhea's vacant look.

"They both died at almost the exact same age," I said, closing the folder. "How is that possible?"

Rhea took a deep breath and leaned back on her hands so she could raise her chin to the sky as she blinked back tears. "My aunt didn't get an autopsy, so we can't be sure."

Those words meant a lot more to her than they did to me. I didn't know the first thing about strokes, except that old people had them. But Rhea's mom? I'd seen pictures. The woman was beautiful and petite. How could she die of a stroke?

"It lists my mom's physician in one of the reports, so I paid her a visit today," she said without any prompting. "I knew she'd remember my mom. Everyone does."

"Yeah," I agreed. I'd only seen a picture and I wouldn't forget that face in my lifetime.

"My mom only came in for antibiotics a few times, but the doctor diagnosed her with bradycardia since my mom's resting heart rate had been around fifty. The doctor said my mom didn't have any of the negative symptoms associated with the bradycardia though, so she let her go. This was several years before my mom died."

I had no idea what bradycardia was, but I wasn't going to interrupt to ask.

"Low heart rates aren't bad," Rhea said, as if reassuring herself. "Most professional athletes have bradycardia and it's considered good. Swimmers can hold their breath for six minutes while free diving, some cyclists have hearts that only beat once every two seconds. It's not a problem for them."

A picture was coming together. Bradycardia had something to do with having a low resting heart rate, which was good for athletes but bad for her mom somehow. I kept my mouth shut, letting Rhea get it all out.

"My mom's doctor took my pulse, listened to my heart and asked me to come in for a heart scan."

This time I had to ask to get an answer since Rhea phased out. "What's your pulse?"

"Forty-two beats per minute."

My medical knowledge may have been next to non-existent, but I knew that was slow. "Forty-two? Lower than your mom's?"

She nodded slowly. "But I'm really active, so the doctor doesn't know if it's congenital or conditioning. Or both."

I opened my mouth to speak, but shut it again when I couldn't think of anything to say that didn't sound completely wrong.

"With my mom, the blood settled in her heart and coagulated," she continued. "It formed a little clot that got knocked loose, traveled up to her brain and caused her to die of a stroke in her sleep."

Words failed me . . . for about two seconds before I blurted, "Do you think that's what happened to your aunt?" The moment the words were out, I wished them back, but Rhea answered anyway.

"Who knows? But it's possible."

She didn't add anything else, staring again at the sets of incoming waves. Yet one other question hung in the air—one she wanted to answer. Or at least it felt that way.

"So . . . ?" How to phrase it? "Does the doctor think you're prone to strokes?"

She gave no indication that she heard my question. Not even blink, but I knew better. The waves crashed several times before she said, "If I stay in shape, she thinks it's highly unlikely. She says my heartbeat is strong and my blood highly oxygenated. If it stays that way, I have nothing to worry about."

There was a big ol' "but" at the end of that sentence that went unsaid about the possibilities on the horizon if Rhea chose not to exercise. Like her mom had.

If Rhea got lazy, her heart might weaken to the point where blood would settle, clot, and kill her.

Perspective was an amazing thing, because suddenly my life wasn't looking so bad.

Next to me, Rhea let out a deep sigh that sounded like it came from the depths of her soul. "Thanks for tracking me down. I needed to say all that out loud. Now it all feels real."

"It's the least I can do," I said, knowing I should mention that it was Ben's concern that had sent me out to find her. She needed to tell him all this. But for some reason I hesitated as her eyes looked me over, as if reassessing me.

"What?" I asked, feeling self conscious.

A careful smile curved her lips. "It's just strange to have a *friend that's a girl, that's all. That conversation with you was totally different than it would have been with Ben."*

Ben finding out that Rhea might die at an early age? Oh yeah. That was a freak-out waiting to happen.

But more important, Rhea had just called me her friend. And she was right. When I needed her, she was there. And when she needed someone, I had been the one she let show up. She needed me, just like I needed her, even though I don't think either of us could point to why, exactly, we trusted each other so blindly.

"You going to tell Ben?" *It went without saying that Rhea would never share another secret with me again if I took it upon myself to inform any other living human of what she'd just told me.*

Rhea laughed. "Not the way I just told you." *She thought about it.* "A variation of the truth," *she decided, sending me a conspiratorial look.* "But it will help that someone knows the whole truth."

I smiled. What else could I do? But at the same time, I knew Rhea had a worried non-boyfriend pacing and waiting for his phone to ring.

"He's worried, you know," *I said, holding up my phone and wiggling it.* "You should call him."

"Yeah," *she breathed, standing and brushing the sand from her pants.* "I guess it's back to the real world now."

* * *

The elevator dinged, and the doors opened to let Rhea and me onto my floor.

"She seriously got her PA a Bentley?" I laughed, as Rhea and I traded Hollywood gossip. "I need to connect with her publicist and see if I can make a connection there."

"Kelly allegedly got him one too," Rhea said. "You should ask him when you have him on the phone." We turned and started to my door when Rhea stopped abruptly. "Rain check on lunch?" she asked, indicating down the hall.

I followed her gaze, knowing from her expression who I would find there. Dahl, sporting a new black eye and a fat upper lip. As uncharitable as it was, I kind of liked seeing him looking messed up.

"I'll call," I said, and she immediately started back to the elevator, disappearing from my peripheral vision while I kept my eyes on Dahl. It took a lot of guts showing up after last night. I had to give that to him. And I was also going to give him an overdue conversation.

Chin high and steps confident, I walked down the hall to meet him.

"I've got to give you points for persistence," I said, unlocking the door and motioning for him to enter. A little bit of my swagger melted away when I noticed all the alcohol I'd bought the day before strewn haphazardly across the bar. Dahl would love that. I glanced at him to see if there was any chance he missed them and found him staring right at the bottles.

"Who was he?" he asked, his voice sounding hard. If we were dating I'd say he sounded jealous, but as things stood I tried not to read into his inflection.

"Long story there," I sighed. "The very oversimplified answer would be to say that he's Rhea's ex."

His face registered shock, which was nice. In all the scenarios he had imagined, he hadn't thought of that possibility. "Rhea dated him?" I might as well have claimed that Donald Trump was Santa Claus.

"Big history there," I confirmed. "Which was why he was staying with me and not at her place."

He considered that. "Why was he here?"

"None of your business," I shot back. "But how about we talk about why every time I open my door, you're standing outside it. I thought you were going to start avoiding me."

He took a deep breath, his eyes not meeting mine. "Friday

night threw me a little bit. I knew you were impaired, and I let you walk out the door with someone . . ."

Another one of his unfinished sentences. "Friday is all on me, Dahl," I said getting a bag for the empty bottles.

Moving across the room with surprising speed, he took the bag from my hands. "Are you saying that I couldn't have stopped you from leaving with that man on Friday?"

He was so close, his Stetson cologne faint but pleasant. "No," I confessed. "If we're being honest here, I wanted you to stop me. But that doesn't mean it was your job to do so. I'm a big girl, Dahl."

His arms encircled me without permission and pulled me into a tight hug. "I have to ask you to forgive me for that, because I'll never forgive myself. I wouldn't have let my worst enemy walk away in that condition, but I convinced myself it was what you wanted."

What I wanted was to stay just as we were for the rest of the day. He'd grabbed me and yanked me against him, and all I felt was warmth. If there was a way to explain to Dahl how significant his touch was to me without freaking him out, I would have done so. As it was, it was clear he was looking for some livable boundaries with me. The best way to create those was with truth.

"Don't blame yourself," I said, pulling away to look at him. "I'm broken, Dahl. And I was broken long before you ever met me, so there's no point in heaping blame on yourself."

His eyebrows drew together in confusion.

"Take a seat," I said, motioning to the couch. "Want some water?" It was all I had that he would drink.

"No, I'm good."

"Fine. Be right back."

I used my time in the kitchen talking myself through what I was planning on sharing with him. I'd never told a guy about what happened back in college. I couldn't help it if someone already knew, but I'd never shared. Dahl needed to know. If I didn't tell him, I would lose someone who was proving to have great friend potential. I could count the men I was comfortable with on one hand, and half of them were in a different state.

Dahl wouldn't tell anyone my secret. And if it made him too uncomfortable, then he really would disappear from my life, and he'd be able to do so knowing that he wasn't the reason I was a head case.

Taking a deep breath, my hand shook as I picked up my glass and went to join Dahl on the couch. No preamble, no delicacy. I just had to lay it out.

"I'm the one who should be apologizing to you, Dahl," I said, dropping in next to him. "I used you, but it was for a really good reason."

"I don't understand," he stammered.

"I don't like men," I confessed, noting that it came out wrong as soon as I said the words. "I'm not gay," I clarified. "But I hate every man I've ever slept with." That sounded even worse. I totally sucked at this.

Dahl blinked, clearly not comprehending even though he was trying.

"You may have noticed that this is my first time telling a guy this, so hang in there with me, okay?"

He nodded.

All I had to do was say it. Get the worst part out at the front without being all dramatic about it. "Once upon a time, I was drugged at a frat party and gang raped by a room full of a men. It kind of tweaked me."

His jaw dropped. "K—"

"No, just let me talk for a second, or I'll lose the courage to explain what this has to do with you." Already I was losing courage. I had to physically close my eyes to start again. "I'd never done more than kiss a guy before going to college. Then after a few weeks on campus, a room full of guys drugged me, hung me up like a piece of meat, and took turns." Whoa. I hadn't meant to say that. Way too personal. Rhea didn't even know that unless she'd deduced it from the reports. And since she was her, she probably had.

"Anyway," I said, skipping ahead. "The point is that even though I was out of it when everything happened, my body has never really forgotten. It doesn't like to be touched. Even if I think I want it, my body will freak out on me, which makes things painful." Only then did I look at him. "I didn't know why until I met you."

He blinked, as if those words stunned him.

"When I kissed you in Jackson Hole, it was a power play on my part. I do that to guys. I give them a taste and hang the possibility of more over their heads. It makes me feel sick, but I always figure it's worth it." Once again, I had to drop my eyes as I watched him grow angrier. "It was supposed to be a quick peck with you, but when I touched you, the weirdest thing happened. I didn't freak out. Nothing hurt, and I didn't know why."

"I sensed something," he breathed, as if that fact were important to him as well. "You seemed . . . shy."

I tried not to let his comment derail me. "That's why I kissed you the other night," I confessed. "I wanted to see if that had been a fluke."

He leaned in, although I wish he hadn't. "Was it?"

I shook my head. "No, I'm comfortable with you. Just like I'm comfortable with Ty and Ben—the guy you met last night." I couldn't help but look at his injuries. "The one that punched you out when you called me easy."

Dahl stood abruptly, pacing away from me.

"I'm telling you all this so you know Friday isn't your fault. I always need to be a little drunk to sleep with a guy. It's not like the first time that's happened, although I'm going to try to avoid idiots like Alan in the future."

"Kathryn," he breathed, turning to face me. I didn't let him finish.

"I'm telling you this because men fall into four categories in my life. Category One are men who are irrelevant. I don't even see them." I ticked the next one off on my finger. "Category Two are men that I charm because I see a future use for them. Category Three," I said, counting off another finger and ignoring his appalled expression. "Men I sleep with and never see again. Or if I do, they know that what we did was a one-shot deal and there's zero chance that they're getting so much as a handshake out of me."

He looked ill, which was appropriate. If what I had done on Friday was so horrific to him, why shouldn't it be sickening to hear that I made a common practice out of it? There had been dozens of Alan Whites in my life.

"And last, Category Four. These are men, like Ben, I'm friends with. No funny business. Just friends. And I told you all this crap because I sense you could fall in that category. Also, because I wanted you to feel completely confident that I won't try to seduce you or anything, since that seems to be a concern with you. And also to arm you with the knowledge that if you were ever tempted to seduce me, I would hate you forever." I paused and made sure he was looking at me. "That's no joke, Dahl. I think of Alan now, and I want to puke. I feel the same about every man I've been with. Friendship is all I got in me."

Unable to handle the horror on his face, I stood and walked to my door, opening it. "I know you came here expecting to be the one to talk. Maybe you were even going to apologize or something. I don't care." I motioned for him to leave. "This is what you got, and I'm going to do you the favor of letting you think it all over before you respond, so I'm going to ask you to leave now."

"But I—"

"Sorry," I interrupted. "If you haven't noticed, my hands are shaking, and I think I might throw up. I would really rather you not be here when that happens, so please go." He hesitated, so I got a little more assertive. "Now."

His steps were reluctant, which was something, at least. Then he stopped and looked down at me when he reached the door. He didn't have a clue what to say. That was obvious. I wouldn't have known what to say if I was him either.

"Are hugs allowed between friends?" he asked.

I nodded. "Yes, but keep in mind I am not feeling well."

There wasn't even a moment's hesitation as he reached out and enfolded me in his arms. Tears bit at my eyes, fighting their way out even as I pushed them back. At least until he left. Tears made guys feel helpless, and I couldn't do that to him at this point.

I memorized the pressure of his arms, his scent, and the feel of his body just in case this was the last time. When his hands moved up to touch my hair, I stepped away.

"Thanks for coming over." I wasn't trying for cold. It just came naturally.

"Yeah," he breathed moving across the threshold. "See you around?"

"That's up to you," I said and shut the door behind him. Then I raced to the bathroom.

TWENTY-THREE

"THANK YOU FOR *seeing me," I enunciated quickly into the mirror. Even when I sped up the pacing of the words, I still held on to the vowels too long. And if I could hear it, an employer could too. "Thank you," I repeated, trying for a smaller sound byte. It didn't help.*

From head to toe, I looked perfect. Hair tamed and sleeked so as not to distract from where I wanted my interviewer to look, which was at my eyes and mouth. For the eye makeup, I'd copied the KABC's anchorwoman's look exactly. For my lips, I'd gone a shade darker than her because I needed the interviewer to listen. After all, if he couldn't listen to me for five minutes, why would he hire me to talk to millions?

Okay, I was getting ahead of myself. It was just an internship. But internships turned into jobs, which is why I needed to dress for the job I was really applying for: news correspondent.

For the pant suit, I'd chosen Calvin Klein because it was conservative, reasonably timeless, and didn't scream high mainte-nance. Under the jacket, I wore a vivid blue top that brought the attention back up to my eyes. For jewelry I stuck with earring studs and Rhea's tree necklace. It had gotten me the job with Imre, so it kind of felt like a good luck charm. The only part of my outfit that implied I had any personality at all were my Betsey Johnson heels.

I'd forced myself to get Rhea's approval before buying them, and they'd received a hearty thumbs up.

Everything was officially perfect except for my voice.

People in California might buy makeup from a girl with a Southern drawl, but I'd also learned that most of them thought "pretty" was the only thing I understood. They heard my accent and immediately assumed I was stupid, no matter what I said.

If I wanted to work as a reporter in Los Angeles, the accent had to go. Either that, or I needed to aim for a career in weather forecasting. No thanks.

"Thank you," I repeated, hearing the problematic diphthongs this time. I stuck them into every vowel that left my mouth, it seemed.

"Thenk." Okay, that sounded weird, but better so I repeated it. The key seemed to be to make vowels as lazy as possible and not open the mouth very far at the same time I cut off the sound. I took a small breath and opened my mouth as little as I could. "You."

It actually sounded right.

Great. Now I just needed to have an interview where all I had to say was "thank you" over and over again. Turning on the TV, I changed the channel until I found some diction tutors on a soap opera.

"Sammy," a dark, chiseled man said in exaggerated horror. "What have you done?"

"Sammy," I repeated, purposefully overdoing his western accent. "What have you done?" I seemed to do great when mocking the accent. Then it struck me: that's exactly what I had to do to fool my interviewer. I had to make fun of how he talked.

Well, if that's how it had to be, then that's how it had to be, because nothing was getting between me and an internship at KABC. There was no way I'd come as far as I had to have anything or anyone get in my way.

* * *

We weren't the first on the scene, which always put me in a

bad mood. At first glance, it looked like Channel 4 had the best angle of the action behind the police line. Other stations were setting up and Channel 13 was right behind us.

"Do you think they found her?" Nick asked.

I flipped the sun visor and checked my makeup. "We only know it's a female body. We don't know if it's tied to a current missing person. I'll find the PIO. You find a tree to climb or a boulder to stand on to see if you can get a peek in there that shows about where they're looking."

"Done," he said, immediately exiting. It was so nice not to have him fighting me anymore.

I studied my reflection in the small mirror. Hair straight, lipstick nude, and another Jason Wu number. George had approved those, and Nick had called the hair and makeup. Market research came back positive on pale lips and tame hair. I'd have to get Isaac to stock me up on straightener.

"Go get 'em," I muttered before pushing the door open and grabbing my notebook.

"PIO?" I asked the first officer I came across.

"Richards," the officer said, moving quickly past.

"Thank you," I said, looking around for the face I knew well as both relief and disappointment washed through me. Dahl had two days left on the force, which meant he could have been PIO, but he wasn't. No biggie. It would have been awkward anyway. I hadn't heard back from him since my tell-all at my apartment. Not one of my more brilliant moments, but for some reason, I didn't regret it. Or maybe I was just too numb at the moment, and it would all hit me later.

Either way, I'd chosen the wrong time to psychoanalyze the situation. I needed to track Richards down to find out if this was breaking news on one of Utah's more infamous cold cases, or just a lead story.

The problem was, the PIO was MIA, and I wasn't the only reporter who had noticed.

Nick had set his camera at the base of a tree and was climbing up it. I decided to head his way to see if he could point me in the right direction when my phone buzzed with a text in my pocket. I took it out, praying for direction.

I stopped walking when I saw it was from Dahl. Looking around the crime scene I wondered if I had somehow missed him in the throng. I still didn't see him, so I settled on reading his text.

Body is unidentifiable. Authorities are going to wait for an autopsy to declare identity.

I immediately called Carla.

"What's the story?" she asked, picking up on the first ring.

"They're not going to speculate on identity. All they're saying is that a body has been found, and they're going to do an autopsy."

"Are you sure?" she hedged. "Four has already preempted The View."

"That's on them, then, because they're not going to have anything to say other than a body was found today and they couldn't wait until noon to announce it."

"Okay," she breathed. "You're live at noon then. Feed us updates."

"Will do," I said, and closed the call.

Where was Dahl, and why had he texted me? Was he already on scene? If so, why wasn't he the PIO?

"Looking for someone?" a deep voice said from behind me. I nearly jumped but managed instead to spin around with a relative amount of sophistication.

I wiggled my phone at him. "Got your text."

"Yeah, I figured what was the point of being a cop for the next two days if I couldn't do a friend a favor or two."

My breath caught as I studied his shy smile for a clue of what he was thinking. "Friend?" I repeated.

"If your offer still stands," he added a little nervously. "I know it's been four days, but they've been busy days. I promise."

"Yeah?" I actually felt a little light headed, but kept my expression normal. "Anything you want to tell me over lunch?"

"Two o'clock?" he ventured.

"Done," I agreed. "Now if you'll excuse me, I have to get back to work."

"By all means," he said, stepping away.

"Oh, and feel free to text me any time," I called after him.

Instead of replying he brought out his phone and typed in a text as he moved back onto the crime scene. A moment later my phone buzzed and I opened it.

I've created a monster, it read. I laughed, catching one last glimpse of him before he disappeared into some trees. I never would have guessed it the first time I met him, but the guy was going to make one good friend. And heaven knew I could use one of those as much as anyone.

"Thank you," I whispered to no one at all and then went to Nick to tell him what I'd found out.

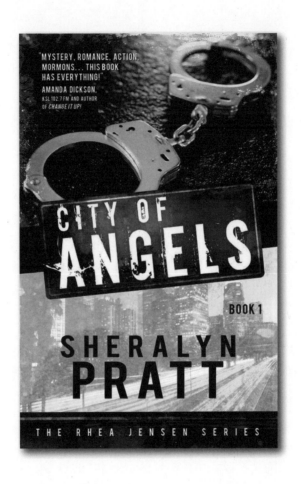

"MYSTERY, ROMANCE, ACTION,
MORMONS... THIS BOOK
HAS EVERYTHING!"
AMANDA DICKSON,
KSL 102.7 FM AND AUTHOR
OF *CHANGE IT UP!*

CITY OF
ANGELS

BOOK 1

SHERALYN
PRATT

THE RHEA JENSEN SERIES

ONE

A **JOYFUL SOB MINGLED** with the happy chatter of birds in the outdoor restaurant. "Yes!" the woman three tables down on my right cried out, just before leaning to drop a kiss on the man kneeling before her. The proposal and acceptance earned a gentle clap from older couples at surrounding tables.

Ah, romance. Something about it brought people together in ways that bank teller lines, traffic jams, and cramped movie theaters couldn't hold a candle to. There was just something about a proposal that made all the witnesses feel like they were friends for the evening, even if they might flip each other off the next day on the freeway.

In truth, the ambience of the outdoor restaurant was perfect for the romantic retelling of a proposal story. Lighting was provided exclusively by the sun or candle light, and the hanging canopies gave every table the illusion of privacy. Very swank. Add that to the fact that Little Bo Peep's was surrounded by lush botanical gardens, and you had the go-to place for creating a cherished memory. Proposals, anniversaries, celebrations . . . things like that.

And my date was late.

"He's fitting the bill so far," Kyp's voice said in my ear. "I especially like the discrete exit ten feet to your left."

I nodded, knowing he could see my acknowledgment from the camera I'd attached to a rose stem directly behind me that was now broadcasting into his van and recording my every move. Turning my attention back to my phone, I pulled up YouTube and typed "handcuff escape" in the search box.

I'd been on a kick recently to find the easiest way out of handcuffs. All considered, if you had the right tool, it was ridiculously easy. Paper clips, bobby pins, playing cards, and a dozen other everyday objects could do the job. I just wanted to find the least conspicuous one before I made the tool that would attach on my favorite bracelet of all time. It was amazing how functional jewelry could be when you put your mind to it.

"One o'clock," Kyp said in my ear. "Waiter with a wine glass and rose. I think this is our guy."

My heart pounded a few times before I settled it down again. Calm. Timid. I had to look like a pushover or my "date" might back out. I wasn't good at meek, so I hoped my new clothes and Pollyanna hair were helping me out on that front. A Norma Kamali long-sleeved empire dress served as my attire that evening. A Walmart special. It screamed, "Poor as dirt, but trying to hide it." Especially compared to the finery surrounding me. The tablecloth was worth more than my dress, for crying out loud. The ill-fitting cut felt awkward when I moved, but I figured it should get the job done.

"Agatha?" the waiter inquired when he reached my table, using the name I'd given out online.

"That's me," I said, trying to put some farm-girl innocence into my eyes.

"I've been asked to bring this to you," the waiter said as he placed the glass and rose in front of me. "Your date has been detained and should be here shortly. He sends his apologies."

"Thank you," I said as I reached for the drink.

"Is there anything else you would like while you are waiting? An appetizer, perhaps?"

Why not? "Sure. How about a glass of water, no ice, and your feta wraps."

He nodded, his eyes taking note of my dress, probably calculating his tip in advance. "I'll bring those right out, ma'am."

I watched him go and then looked down at the white wine in front of me. From a distance it might look like water, especially in poor lighting, and that's exactly what I was banking on. But first I needed to make sure I had my smoking gun. Reaching into my purse, I pulled out a packet of little strips. The sole purpose of my strips was to test for two of the most popular date-rape drugs, which were also the drugs the man I was hunting had used on his previous victims: ketamine and gamma hydroxybutyrate, aka GHB.

The test is simple, really. You drip a part of your drink onto the tester strip. If it turns blue, you know you're in trouble. If it doesn't, all is well.

"What's the verdict?" Kyp asked even though we both knew the answer. This guy wasn't varying his MO. He thought that using different restaurants and finding girls on different Internet sites kept him safe. Maybe it would have, but he'd messed with the wrong girl along the way. And that girl's dad had hired me.

"Blue," I said, dropping the strip into my purse and picking up my phone. *Little Bo Peep's,* I typed into a new text. *Pick up case summary on right rear tire. It's going down now. Tag. You're it.* After pressing "send," I set the phone down on the table.

Lifting the glass, I swirled the liquid, supposedly to check for residue, as I calculated what to do next. My guy was already at the restaurant. He had to be. It was the only explanation for my drink being drugged, because I wasn't buying for an instant that the waiter had been slipped a twenty to do the deed.

So Mr. Bad was here and most likely watching me. I would have been watching me if I were him. Was he at the bar or peeping through one of the windows from the main building? Had he ordered the drink as if he were going to bring it to me himself and then pretended to chicken out and asked the waiter to do it for him while he pulled himself together? The drink only needed to be unattended for two seconds for him to do what he needed to. No one would suspect a thing.

I really needed the waiter to come back with my order, but in the meantime, I got ready for the switch. I had a little thermos for the wine in the Manhattan-sized handbag I'd picked up with the dress. I removed the thermos and hid it in my lap, ready to capture the wine as evidence. Now I just had to figure out how I was going to do it, seeing as how my "date's" eyes were undoubtedly glued on me by this point, and anything suspicious might scare him off. On the other hand, it was April, and the sun was already disappearing behind the horizon. It was nearly dark. What if he just couldn't see me for a moment? The entire place was candlelit, and I was in a corner with rose bushes, so I didn't have to be worried about being backlit.

The plan was still formulating when the waiter returned.

"Your wraps, ma'am, and a water with no ice."

"Thank you. This will be great."

He looked hesitant to leave. "I'm sure your date will be here soon," he said apologetically. I smiled, regarding him as a witness and wanting him to remember everything as clearly as possible. I shot him a lazy smile.

"He's ten minutes late," I said, checking my watch. "Would you keep me waiting that long?"

He swallowed. "No, ma'am, I don't think I would."

Really? Even with my hair like this? He was blushing. How cute. "Tell me," I continued. "Should I wait? Do you think this guy is worth waiting for?"

His focus shifted to the side, and I could tell he was recalling the man who sent me the drink. When he looked back at me, he gave a small shake of his head. "I think you can do much better, ma'am."

I let my eyes warm as I gave him a once-over. "Well, thanks for thinking so."

He nodded and stepped away, not knowing I had just permanently sketched the face of my perp into his brain.

"Should I call the police?" Kyp asked.

"Not until he shows himself," I muttered, trying not to move my lips.

Kyp didn't like my reply. "The guy drugged your drink. That's grounds enough to arrest him. Why shouldn't we call the police? The waiter knows who he is."

I sighed. Some people had no sense of adventure. "Still, wait until I've secured the suspect. It's more tidy that way."

"Rhea, that's the police's job," he cautioned.

"If the police show up, he'll bolt. We've got to close the deal now."

I heard him sigh. "The police aren't going to like you today."

They never did. "Ready?" I said, then conveniently sneezed right onto the candle as my hands dumped the wine into the thermos, twisting the lid on and dropping it back in my purse. I stood, motioning for the waiter to re-light my candle while pouring some of the water from my regular glass into the wine glass to replace what I'd dumped. It took less than five seconds, which hopefully wouldn't spook my guy. Time would tell.

Once my candle was glowing again, I tested my water in the wine glass, just to be sure, and found it drug-free. I downed it, grabbed a feta wrap and my phone, and settled in to wait for my guy while watching some man with a German accent on YouTube explain how to use two paper clips to make handcuff keys for police-grade cuffs. I already knew that one.

"Are you timing me?" I asked Kyp, not looking up.

"Yeah, we're at five."

According to my research, it was reasonable for me to show strong reactions by the ten-minute mark. And with me sitting and given my low body weight, going to sleep was a distinct possibility. Softening my body language, I tried to give the impression I was going lax while watching a kid escape trick cuffs. It went against my instincts not to keep an eye on my environment, but that's what Kyp was for. He was my eyes so I could play my part and not clue this guy into who he was dealing with.

Deciding YouTube had nothing for me, I shut down my browser and placed the phone in my purse while casually pulling out my police-grade cuffs and setting them in my lap under the table.

One minute later, I started blinking drowsily. When Kyp whispered, "Ten," in my ear, I let my head fall to the side. The stage was set. The question was, would my date bite?

"Incoming," Kyp whispered just before I heard footsteps. They stopped at my table and paused a moment before someone blew out the candle lighting my table. My corner was officially dark, and my pounding heart had started the job of pumping adrenaline into my system. The footsteps moved behind me, and the side gate to my left squeaked open, propped open by a rock. No one around us noticed my date's motions, focusing instead on their hushed conversations.

"I knew it," Kyp hissed, and I could tell he wanted to beat this man into the ground. We both read the reports. He knew as well as I the state he had left his previous "dates" in. One false move and I would happily take this guy down myself.

Coming to my side, my suspect caressed my face and spoke.

"You don't look anything like your picture, Agatha." His voice was intimate, soft, almost seductive. He pinched my arm and I nearly flinched. He was testing to see if I was faking and nearly succeeded in outing me. Underneath the tablecloth my left hand gripped the cuffs. "You're very strong," he said, stroking my arm. "Why do women today try to make themselves into men?"

In one motion I placed the heel of my right palm across the back of his hand, pushing his hand toward his wrist as I stood and cranking his arm behind his back until he was standing on his tippy toes, instinctively positioning himself so I wouldn't break his wrist.

"We're strong so we can protect ourselves against men like you," I said, snapping one of the cuffs on his wrist. He tried to struggle, but did not cry out when I kicked the back of his knees to make him fall forward. When his other arm flailed to fight for balance, I caught it, yanked it back with his other one, and cuffed it as well. I looked around, making sure no one had noticed us. They hadn't. We were just a lone couple in a dark corner while the rest of the establishment ate on.

"You do so much as take a deep breath and I will break you," I whispered into the man's ear. "Do you understand?" To my dismay, he didn't even offer a token resistance. He just nodded like a man who'd been praying to be caught. I liked it better when they fought.

Leaning away, I spoke again, keeping my voice soft. "Kyp, have you called the police?"

"I'm talking to them now."

"Tell them I'm taking him out the back gate and we'll wait for them by the pepper gardens." Maybe I'd make the guy eat a few while we were waiting. Some were strong enough to make an elephant cry.

"Should we bring an ambulance?" Kyp asked. "Did you break anything?"

"Not a scratch," I replied, looking over the man that had brought so much heartache into the world. Dark hair, receding hairline, normal face. Just your average, everyday guy trying not to hyperventilate. Why couldn't sick men like him just walk around wearing a sign or grow the same facial hair or something?

"Fine," Kyp said. "I'll get the camera and meet you once I get off the phone with them."

"I'll be waiting," I said, wrapping my hand around my date's thumb and pushing the bone straight into the hand joint until he gasped in pain. I had his attention. "We're going to leave quietly now. Do you understand?"

When his head nodded vigorously, I pushed a little harder so he wouldn't get any ideas. "Okay, stand on three. Ready? One, two, three."

He stood, no tricks, and was as docile as a lamb as I led him out the back gate and kicked the rock away from the door to let the gate shut behind us. When I reached out to stop the door from clattering shut and disturbing the diners, he made his move. It was smart of him to wait until I was multitasking, but it was also very predictable. When he chose to rush me rather than just run, I think it was his goal to smash me against the fence and daze me before running for it. Or maybe he hadn't thought that far in advance. I'd never ask, but it was easy enough to twist out of his way and let him run face first into the fence before spinning him around and dropping a strike on the top of his sternum. Air rushed out of him in a sob as he sunk to his knees and fought to remember how to breathe in again. He'd figure it out.

"Upsie daisy," I said, pushing up on a nerve bundle in his armpit. "I said we'd be by the peppers so we've got a little ways to go."

Breaths tripping over each other, the man stood and stumbled forward as I pushed from behind. Kyp and the police would be along any minute and relieve me of this guy, but long before I heard either of them, I heard something infinitely more familiar. It was the voice of a woman I'd known since college, saying:

"This is Kathryn McCoy, coming to you live from a small restaurant in Pasadena, where a serial-rapist has just been apprehended . . ."

Tag, Kay, I thought. *You're so it.*

*S*HERALYN PRATT GRADUATED from the University of Utah with a BA in Communication. She loves travel, well-trained dogs, good sushi, and is a sucker for rice krispy treats. To learn more about upcoming projects or to gain insights into the Rhea Jensen series, visit Sheralyn online at www.sheralynpratt.com or follow her on twitter: @sheralynpratt.